Love Off-Limits

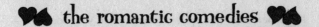

the romantic comedies

Love Off-Limits

WHITNEY LYLES

Simon Pulse
New York London Toronto Sydney

SIMON PULSE
An imprint of Simon & Schuster Children's Publishing Division
1230 Avenue of the Americas, New York, NY 10020
First Simon Pulse paperback edition August 2009
Copyright © 2009 by Whitney Lyles
All rights reserved, including the right of reproduction in whole or in part in any form.
SIMON PULSE and colophon are registered trademarks of Simon & Schuster, Inc.
For information about special discounts for bulk purchases, please contact Simon & Schuster Special Sales at 1-866-506-1949 or business@simonandschuster.com.
The Simon & Schuster Speakers Bureau can bring authors to your live event. For more information or to book an event contact the Simon & Schuster Speakers Bureau at 1-866-248-3049 or visit our website at www.simonspeakers.com.
Designed by Ann Zeak
The text of this book was set in Garamond 3.
Manufactured in the United States of America
10 9 8 7 6 5 4 3 2 1
Library of Congress Control Number 2009920687
ISBN: 978-1-4169-7508-3

For my daughter Lyla,
who was with me the whole time

Acknowledgments

Hugs and thanks to my wonderful agent, Elise Capron. I couldn't ask for a better agent and am forever grateful for all her support, wisdom, and guidance. Thanks also to the entire SDLA team, who continues to keep wind in my sails.

Thank you to Sangeeta Mehta, who gave this book a pulse—no pun intended. Special thanks to my sharp editor, Michael del Rosario, for really bringing the book to life with his invaluable feedback and fine-tuning.

Thanks to all friends, family, and fans who continue to cheer for me. In particular, Rob and Charlotte, Mom, Dad, Jen, Chip, Carol, Doug, and Annie.

A note to my daughter Lyla, whose life has run an interesting parallel to this novel. Shortly after I received the news that I would be publishing another Romantic Comedy, I learned that I was expecting another daughter. In fact, my due date for delivering the manuscript was only days away from my pregnancy due date.

Writing is often a very lonely profession. However, I could feel Lyla's kicks and hiccups for the entire duration of writing this novel. Thanks to Lyla for giving me the gift of company.

One

Dear Coyote Courtship,

I've wanted to ask this girl to the Halloween dance all year, but I'm not sure if she even likes me. Should I talk to her friends before I ask her? Or should I just ask her?

Sincerely,
Confused Coyote

There were a million more Confused Coyotes.

Dear Coyote Courtship,

I really like this guy, but I'm afraid to ask him to the dance. I know he doesn't have a date yet, and he'd probably say yes, but I feel so intimidated. I am really shy. I'm afraid he'll get a date soon if I don't do something. Any suggestions on how to ask him as casually as possible?

Yours truly,
Chicken

And a lot of Chickens.

Hi, Coyote Courtship,

I really want to ask a friend to the dance, but I'm afraid he might take it the wrong way. How do I make it clear that I just want to be friends?

Thanks for the advice.
Just Friends

Several friendly coyotes apparently hung out on campus, because she read a few more letters similar to Just Friends's.

The dilemmas were endless. Natalie Dean never knew one dance could create such anguish for so many people. She'd almost rather take driver's ed again than read the pile of letters from anonymous classmates that sat in front of her in the campus newsroom. All the letters were for the school newspaper's column that she'd taken over when the former love columnist had quit.

The campus newsroom was empty. The only sound was the hum of the computer she was using and the occasional grunts and shouts from the Coyote football practice outside. Even though October was right around the corner, it still felt like summer in their suburban San Diego town, and the warm breezes wafting through the windows made Natalie want to take a nap.

She began typing.

—*The Coyote Chronicle*—

COYOTE COURTSHIP

It's the season of spooks, and we're all hoping to avoid messages from beyond the grave. With one of the biggest events on campus, Howl at the Moon, right around the corner, many of you are hoping to make this season full of fun rather than fright. I've received a lot of letters asking about how to hook the best date for the dance. *I'm dying to ask the one I've had a crush on all year, but I'm afraid. Should I take a friend? Is it okay to head to the dance with a group of friends? I want the one I've had my eye on all year to ask me; how do I get her attention?*

3

The fact of the matter is, I don't have a clue, and frankly I don't care because I wish I wasn't even going to this stupid dance, and anyone who has written in for advice should read their horoscope or contact Dr. Phil. My advice: Avoid love like the plague. Romance is confusing, and if you do think you ever happen to stumble upon true love, eventually you'll end up wondering if it's true or not.

Natalie giggled. She couldn't help it. It was hard to take the column seriously. When she'd first taken over the column, the idea of giving advice had seemed exciting. She'd never admit this, but it had kind of made her feel important and all-knowing. At the time, her own love life had been going blissfully, and she'd savored writing about romance. But lately the column had become a burden. Her relationship with her boyfriend was a source of anguish, and she was starting to feel as though she knew nothing about love when she was supposed to know everything about love. Worse, she'd even secretly been seeking love advice for her own love life via the Internet on a huge love-advice website called Romeohelpme.com. Every time she sat down to work on the column, she felt like the biggest poseur.

She looked over her shoulder. School had been out for more than an hour and she'd been alone in the newsroom. However, paranoia always kicked in when she was screwing around, and she was private about her writing anyway. Her identity as columnist for Coyote Courtship was top secret. The only people on the entire newspaper staff who knew her identity were the newspaper adviser, Mr. Moore, and the editor in chief, Matt Logan. It was so on the down low she wasn't even supposed to work on the column at school, and she had to sign a contract with Mr. Moore promising that she wouldn't tell anyone except for her parents that she was the columnist behind Coyote Courtship. If she violated the agreement, it could result in her failure of the class. That's how seriously everyone took this column—everyone except for her.

The only reason Natalie was working in the newsroom today was because she'd been uploading too many songs on freebie websites and her computer at home had taken a hit from some kind of virus.

The first issue of the newspaper for the school year had hit stands a week earlier, which meant that new deadlines had been issued this week. A first draft of the column was due every Thursday after the previous paper hit stands. She'd sort of come to dread Thursdays for this reason. Love and romance were the most confusing topics on the planet for her right now. She'd rather solve equations than try to figure out dating and relationships, and she was supposed to be an expert!

She knew what all the fans of the column wanted to hear. She'd watched all the fairy-tale movies, and it wasn't like happy endings and blissful advice about romance were rocket science.

She glanced at the clock. She cracked her knuckles over the keyboard of her computer and chuckled. She was about to delete her fake column when the sound of skateboard wheels in the newsroom startled her. She swung around in her seat. *Jeremy.* Detention must be out. She wasn't sure what had surprised her more—the fact that he was a half hour early, or the fact that he had skateboarded into the campus newsroom wearing a fireman's costume.

His dark hair peeked from beneath the edges of his hat; his deep-set eyes scanned

6

the room. Jeremy wore his confidence well and he always seemed so secure in every new setting he entered. He was the only person she knew who had the courage to rip across campus in a Halloween costume as if he were in his backyard. Skateboarding on campus was so against the rules.

Jeremy's Ford Explorer was currently in the shop, and he was waiting for Natalie to give him a ride home from school.

"I've come to the rescue!" he announced as he glided over the floor, avoiding a stack of newspapers.

A million thoughts at once. What was he doing in the outfit? And he was early. She thought he had detention before the Halloween flea market. She was too worried he would catch a glimpse of her sarcastic column to find out why he was early. However, she couldn't help but notice how cute he looked. Really, he was drop-dead gorgeous in anything he wore, but the fireman costume really took his broad shoulders and deep, dark eyes to a new level. Even a cat would love to be rescued by him.

Her mind raced, and all she could think was to get her mouse to the close button or the minimize icon—whichever came faster.

He was the last person she wanted to see her silly attempt to amuse herself. He had no idea that she felt so confused in their relationship, and this definitely wasn't the way she wanted him to find out. She hit minimize faster than her heart raced. The column disappeared.

"What's the matter with you?" he asked as he hopped off his new skateboard. He straightened his fireman's hat.

"Nothing," she said a little too quickly.

He gave her a once-over. "You look startled and you're sweating."

"I am? I mean, hey, look at you!" She turned the focus on him. "Shouldn't I be asking what's up with *you*?" She put on an enthusiastic smile. "I know it's fire season in San Diego, but I didn't know you were signing on to help out."

He seemed excited by her interest. He tossed her a giant black-and-white ball of fur. "I just found these costumes at the Halloween flea market. Five bucks for both. I got the Dalmatian for you."

Natalie held up the giant costume and looked at a head-to-toe dog costume complete with a collar and a tag that read BUSTER.

"Buster?" she mumbled. She didn't want

to hurt his feelings, but this was hardly her vision for this year's Howl at the Moon.

The school held its annual Halloween flea market every year in the gym. It gave the students and staff a chance to recycle some old costumes. Natalie had skipped this year and sent Jeremy to see if he could find something cool for them, or just come up with ideas. She had no idea he would actually buy something without asking her first. He looked wonderful as a firefighter, but going as man's best friend was hardly what she'd had in mind for herself. Did he plan to lead her around on a leash? Not to mention it was eighty degrees outside and could hit the upper nineties on Halloween. This was San Diego. Visions of heat stroke danced through her mind.

"Try it on!" he urged.

"Uh. Well . . ." She searched for a reason to skip his suggestion.

"Bathroom's right next door," he reminded her.

"You want me to try it on right now? Um . . . it doesn't look like it will fit. It's a little large." For once her short frame seemed like a blessing. "Who sold you this?" she asked.

"Mrs. Green. She said it was her son's."

"Is her son Hurley from *Lost*?"

Jeremy laughed. "C'mon. Go try it on. It will look great."

"Let's just wait till we get home. I'll try it on at my house. There are better mirrors there."

"What's wrong with you? Don't be such a chicken. Go try it on."

Jeremy never understood embarrassment, and she doubted he'd experienced a self-conscious moment in his entire life. Always so confident, he felt comfortable in anything. He was daring and bold, and those were two of the qualities that had attracted her to him in the first place. Natalie had always felt safest tucked behind her computer working on a writing assignment. With Jeremy there was never a dull moment. He made everything seem so easy.

He grabbed her arm and yanked her from the seat.

"What if someone comes in," she said, "and I'm standing here in a dog costume?"

"School's been out for more than an hour. Who do you think is going to see you? It will look great, anyway. Just go try it on. What are you waiting for?"

She stood there.

"Nat, no one is here. Just go." He whimpered like a dog. "Please."

She smiled. "All right, all right."

As she headed to the girls' bathroom, she reasoned that it was better to try it on now and let him see how ginormous it was going to be. Maybe he could even get his money back from Mrs. Green or try to sell it at the next Halloween flea market.

She went straight for the handicapped stall. She was afraid she'd get trapped in a regular-size stall. As she slid the outfit on over her clothes, she thought about the fact that people who worked at Disneyland got paid to wear outfits like this. She wouldn't take a king's ransom to wear this to Howl at the Moon. She was afraid to leave the stall and already felt her armpits growing damp. She almost tripped over the costume's legs as she maneuvered her way out of the stall. As predicted, she was swimming in the costume. She looked at herself in the mirror and didn't know whether to laugh or cry. She wanted to put her tail between her legs.

Mainly she was just worried someone was going to walk in and see her. The ears came down to her neck and she looked poufy.

Her face looked like a tiny speck of land in the midst of a giant sea of black and white. For a moment she debated taking it off and explaining that it didn't fit and her cheeks were squished. Leaving the bathroom and walking into daylight terrified her. She knew if she chickened out, Jeremy would never let her hear the end of it. Besides, he was her boyfriend and pretty much the only person she really needed to worry about looking cute for. He wanted her to wear it.

Natalie headed back to the newsroom. An ear flapped over her eye. As she pushed the ear away she heard laughter. Worse, her boyfriend wasn't alone. She faced her boyfriend and his best friend, Matt. Matt also happened to be the editor in chief of the *Coyote Chronicle*. She wanted to die. She sort of wished it had been anyone else.

"This is classic!" Jeremy shouted before succumbing to a no-breather.

Matt looked at her with a twist of sympathy and humor in his blue eyes.

Slowly she took a few steps forward. As she moved, she felt her tail take out a chair. She turned to her left to look at the chair, and when she moved, her tail knocked over something else. Judging from the shattering sound that followed, it was safe to say that whatever had fallen wasn't another chair. She was afraid to move and peeked over her shoulder. A pile of broken gray fragments lay beneath the tail.

"What was that?" She was afraid of the answer.

"Just Matt's ceramics project," Jeremy said in between peals of laughter.

"No. Are you serious?" She prayed Jeremy was kidding, but something told her he wasn't.

Matt tried to act like he didn't mind, but she sensed a shadow of disappointment in his eyes. He shrugged. "It's not a big deal. Just some dumb vase that probably would've broken when my mom put flowers in it anyway."

"It was a vase for your mom?" She felt horrible, and immediately crouched down and began picking up the pieces. "Maybe we can put it back together. I am so sorry. I feel terrible. I mean, was this something you worked on for a long time? This was special, wasn't it?"

Matt shook his head. "Nah, it was just some little school project."

"That he got an A on," Jeremy pointed

out. "I don't think you're going to be able to glue two pieces of that back together." Jeremy's cell phone rang. Natalie was thankful for the interruption, and felt relieved when he turned away to answer it. He was only making her feel worse.

Matt crouched down next to her.

"Let me clean it up," he said. "Really, it's no big deal."

"Is there some way I can make this up to you?"

"It's okay, Buster." He smiled at her while on his hands and knees.

She glanced down at the collar and tag around her neck and rolled her eyes. "Oh yeah." She felt self-conscious and awkward beneath his gaze.

Sweat trickled down her back as she collected pieces of the vase from the floor. Unfortunately, Jeremy was right. The vase looked like a pile of cookie crumbs.

"I should've never agreed to try on this stupid costume in the first place," she mumbled.

"You look hot," Matt said. She paused to glance at him. "I mean, not that kind of hot." He quickly corrected himself. "The hot where you sweat and you want to cool down.

Not that you aren't hot or anything . . . I mean, just never mind. You know what I mean."

Interesting that he was the one stumbling over his words when she felt like the fool. Not only was she crawling around in a dog costume that was ten sizes too big, but she didn't normally hang out in the newsroom to begin with. He was probably dying to know what she was doing here.

They threw handfuls of clay fragments in the trash, and Natalie felt horrible with every toss.

She never worked in the newsroom.

"I was working on the column," she blurted out. "I didn't have a chance to tell you and Mr. Moore that my computer at home is broken, but I have a deadline on Thursday." She tried to sound nonchalant. "My brother's fixing my computer tonight. So I won't be in here anymore after that. I mean, I'll be in here for newspaper stuff . . . just not to write." She was babbling now, and she prayed he didn't ask to have a sneak peek at the column.

"Okay." He ran his fingers through his curly hair. "If your computer breaks down again, you can always borrow mine. I don't care if you come to my house. It's better than someone finding out who you are."

"Thanks. I would've borrowed Jo's, but she has a paper due."

"How's the column going?" he asked.

"Don't worry. I'll have something in time for the Halloween issue of the paper."

Matt shrugged. "I wasn't worried. With you, Nat, I know I never have to worry."

If he only knew how ironic that sounded to her. She'd much rather be writing about the lack of vegetarian choices on the cafeteria menu, or even *writing* the cafeteria menu, for that matter. Or other things she felt passionate about, like, what was the whole point of algebra? Someone had yet to explain this to her. Really, what was the point? And why did she have to understand the meaning of the little letter x?

Matt put his hand on her shoulder. "Thanks for taking this on, Nat. You're doing an awesome job, and I really couldn't picture anyone but you doing this."

She forced a smile. If he only knew the truth.

TWO

After Jeremy and Natalie left the newsroom, they headed to Natalie's house. They
wanted food, and for whatever reason Jeremy
believed they would find a treasure trove of
after-school snacks at Natalie's. The reality
was that Natalie's younger twin brothers,
Thomas and Brandon, gobbled up anything
good within hours of a trip to the grocery store. Natalie figured the main reason
Jeremy had wanted to hang out at her house
as opposed to his was because of his parents' separation and all the strange feelings
involved with his dad moving out.

Today was their lucky day. Apparently
her mother had really stocked up at the
store, and the pantry was full of treats like

Doritos and English muffins. The fridge revealed an assortment of Go-Gurt, string cheese, and cold drinks. While they dined on string cheese and chips, the twins bombarded Jeremy with questions about his new skateboard and what he thought about the last Chargers game while attempting to wrestle with him.

Occasionally Jeremy took a break from his after-school feast to wrestle one of her brothers to the ground.

Saying that her brothers loved Jeremy was an understatement. "Worship" came to mind. They idolized him. Her brothers were complete opposites: Brandon was just like Jeremy, athletic and competitive, but even Thomas the computer whiz was enamored with Jeremy's charisma and capability to do anything.

Really, her whole family was in complete awe of Jeremy. Her mother and grandmother thought he was "so handsome," and her father always seemed to vibe with him about sports and other such guy things. Even her grandmother's dog seemed to fall under Jeremy's spell. Both her parents were at work, and her grandmother was upstairs taking a nap with her dog, Prints William.

Otherwise they would've been in the living room too, gathered around Jeremy as though they were in Antarctica and he was the only source of warmth. Maybe that was why Jeremy liked to come to her house so much. Here he was treated like a celebrity.

"Jeremy." Brandon poked at him.

"Jeremy." Thomas poked on the other arm, competing for attention.

"Jeremy, Jeremy, Jeremy" was all she'd heard since she walked in the front door. It was like listening to a CD skip. The sound got annoying fast and it needed to be changed.

Natalie decided to announce that Jeremy had a new name. "You guys," she called to her little brothers. "Give Jeremy a moment to breathe. And how many times are you going to say his name? Today he has a new name. He's only responding to . . ." She thought for a moment. "Frederick."

"Frederick?" The twins looked puzzled.

"What's up with that?" Jeremy asked. "At least give me something cool, like Chief or Slash."

"No. It's Frederick."

"Frederick, will you show us how you

can go down our patio stairs on your skate-board?" Brandon asked.

Thomas put in his request. "And then play that one song on the piano you made up about when your mom makes something crappy for dinner."

There wasn't anything Jeremy couldn't do. He was even a composer of humorous music.

"Please, Jeremy," Thomas said.

"Ah!" Natalie called him out. "It's Frederick. He can't respond to anything other than Frederick."

"Please, Frederick."

. "It's not Frederick. Frederick sounds like a guy with his pants pulled up too high who collects stamps. It's Slash," Jeremy said.

"Please, Slash."

Instead of going outside, Jeremy hopped on their piano bench and began singing "Natalie loves Hurley from *Law-hawst*! Natalie loves Hurley from *Laaaaw-hawst*!" while playing "Chopsticks." Her brothers fell to the floor with laughter.

Natalie rolled her eyes.

They sang around the piano for a few more minutes before heading outside to watch Jeremy Frederick Slash skateboard down the patio stairs. Natalie stayed behind and looked at the latest issue of the *Coyote Chronicle* for the twenty millionth time. A copy was still sitting on her parents' coffee table. It was starting to look as though someone had been using it as a coaster. Evidence of cold soda cans and glasses of water covered the front page. It didn't matter, though. A dozen other copies could be found around the house, and both her proud parents took several copies to work to show off her non-column articles to their friends.

Natalie looked at Coyote Courtship. It was weird reading the column. Her advice sounded so solid. How could she be dishing out that kind of advice when she didn't even know if she liked her boyfriend anymore?

Dear Coyote Courtship,
    I am dating a guy who is really nice, but I am just not into him anymore. I don't want to hurt his feelings and I still want to be friends. How do I break up with him?
    Yours truly,
    Heartbreaker

Dear Coyote Courtship,
    My boyfriend of ten months recently broke up with me. I am heartbroken. No

matter what I do I can't stop thinking about him. He has totally moved on, and there is no hope for us. How do I heal a broken heart?

Sincerely,
Brokenhearted Me

Coyote Courtship says . . .

Breaking up is never easy, my friends. That's why there are a million sad, slow songs devoted to the subject. Wouldn't life be simple if it were one big fairy tale? If we found the one we were meant to be with on the first shot, and rode happily into the sunset? Unfortunately, that's not how life works, and we're probably all going to be a heartbreaker or heal from a broken heart at least once in our lives. But the bottom line is that breakups are usually for the best. It might be hard to realize at the time, but when something isn't meant to be, it will end up better for you in the long run.

Here are a few good pointers to keep in mind when you're the one breaking a heart:

- Honesty is always the best policy. Be kind, but don't string the other person along.
- Talk to your soon-to-be ex before you tell all your friends you're going to break up with him or her. Be respectful. The person you're breaking up with is likely to feel humiliated as it is, so keep it as private as possible.
- Don't ever break up with someone in public. Give that person a place to cry and express his or her feelings.

When you are the one dealing with a broken heart, time is the most valuable thing. The healing process may be slow, but here are a few suggestions to make the journey less painful.

- Occupy yourself with things that will make you feel stronger about the situation and steer clear of things that will only intensify the pain. For example, turn to Pink. I don't mean the color. I mean the singer. Make a playlist of songs that will make you feel empowered. Pink has a ton of hits devoted to the topic. Don't turn to old photos and cry over his sweatshirt that he left in your car, which leads me to the next pointer.

- Get rid of any memorabilia—for instance, that sweatshirt. Have a friend give it back if it will be too hard to see the person.
- Hang out with your best buds. Go to the movies, eat lots of ice cream, play video games, shop—anything to keep your mind off the breakup.

Whatever situation you're in—whether you're heartbroken or heartbreaking—keep in mind that everything happens for a reason. The reason may not present itself now, but it will eventually. Best of luck.

She'd made it sound so easy. If it was so easy, why couldn't she take a break from her own boyfriend? Because her situation was far too complicated. It wasn't just that her family would adopt Jeremy if they could. Another big reason was that his parents had recently separated. Up until his parents had separated, she had thought Jeremy was actually drifting from her. But lately he'd seemed to need her.

He'd reached out to her more than ever. She couldn't kick the guy while he was down.

The back door flew open, and her brothers came trailing in behind him.

"Okay, Slash has to go now," Jeremy said.

"Can you come over every day, Slash?" Thomas asked.

"Sure, I'd love to."

An hour later Natalie found herself sitting on the ground outside Bank of America watching Jeremy glide on his new skateboard down a ramp meant for wheelchairs, which wasn't exactly how she'd pictured spending the rest of the day. *Let's see,* she thought. Homework and laundry sounded more exciting. Not to mention she felt like she needed to visit her new favorite website, Romeohelpme. She'd been driving Jeremy home when he'd spotted the ramp and asked her to pull into the bank "really quick." Really quick had turned into forty-five minutes. She knew it was only a matter of time before security came and busted her boyfriend and the two other skateboarding friends that he'd made outside the bank.

Fall was typically a warm season in Oak Canyon, and today was no exception. The heat made her feel tired and lazy, and she longed to go home and take a nap. Instead, she decided to text her best friend, Jo. Maybe Jo was finished with her Howl at the Moon committee meeting by now. She found her cell phone in the small pocket of her backpack.

Where r u? Call me.

She waited, praying Jo was around to dish.

Can't call right now. Debating colors for the backdrop at dance. Don't you think we should go with something new, like all black and a big dark blue full moon in the background? Everyone wants the same old orange and black. Call u as soon as I leave. XO.

Natalie wrote back.

Luv the full moon idea.

Then she sent a text to her next-best friend, Vincent. Natalie, Jo, and Vincent had been friends for as long as Natalie could remember. When they were little kids, they'd lived on the street where Natalie currently resided. Then Jo's father had launched his construction business and her family had upgraded to a more posh neighborhood encased by coded gates and palm trees. Vincent's parents had divorced, sending him to a condominium complex with his mother.

Hey Vinny! What are you doing? I'm bored. Call me.

She was the only one who called him Vinny, just like he was the only one who called her Natty. Jo had never really taken to their nicknames. She thought Vinny sounded so Italian mafia and Natty reminded her of "naughty." Her phone beeped. Vincent was one of the best at replying to text messages. She could always count on him for a speedy response.

Can't talk now, Natty. Auditioning for South Pacific. Let's chat L8R.

She felt relieved when Jeremy began to skate her way. She was ready to head home.

She wondered if her computer was back in action and what her mom was making for dinner. He slowed down, leaned over, and plucked a white flower from a planter near the bank. He picked up speed again and came to a scraping halt at her feet.

"It's for you." It seemed like it had been a long time since he'd given her a flower. It was a sweet gesture and made the fact that she'd been sweating her tush off in the heat for what seemed like an eternity seem sort of worthwhile. What girl didn't like to get flowers from her boyfriend, even if the flower was pilfered from a bank's planter? She couldn't help but think back to the days when she'd shown up to school and Jeremy would be waiting by her locker with a rose he'd "borrowed" from someone's front yard. Her heart would race and she'd tell herself that whomever he'd taken it from had a million more to spare. She was easy to please in that way. Flowers, little notes left on her windshield or her locker—the small things made her happy. She didn't need extravagant gifts or expensive dates.

As she took the daisy she felt a little pang of butterflies again. It was a welcome feeling, and it was moments like these that made her want to never let go of him. "Thank you." She smelled the inside and didn't think it really had a scent, but its white petals and purple center looked pristine. "That was sweet of you."

"Did you see me catch air off that ramp? I probably caught five feet!" He seemed so excited.

She nodded, even though she wasn't sure if she remembered. "That was cool."

"You ready to roll?"

She stood up.

"Can I have my sunglasses?" he asked.

She dug inside her purse. "Don't forget your iPod, too." She found the iPod first. When she pulled the sunglasses out, she quickly realized that one of the lenses was cracked. "Oh no," she said.

"You broke my shades?" he asked loudly.

"I didn't break your sunglasses." Her tone was defensive as she watched him check out the damage. "I didn't even touch them," she said.

"They were in *your* purse."

"All I've been doing is sitting here watching you skateboard. I haven't even moved!"

"Well, they weren't like this before I gave them to you."

How could he be Mr. Skateboarding Flower Delivery Man one minute and then so annoying the next? As if she deliberately broke his sunglasses. She hadn't done more than yawn and text Jo since they'd arrived. In fact, she'd been sitting in the heat watching him ollie off the sidewalk ramps, and if he thought he'd caught five feet of air, he was wrong. It looked more like five inches! If anyone had broken his sunglasses, it was him. He was so hard on everything, always breaking things; he'd probably dropped them during one of his skateboarding stunts and hadn't even known a crack had started to form. He was so annoying sometimes.

"Are you sure they weren't like that before? I mean, you're kind of rough with everything. How many pairs of sunglasses do you think you've lost or broken in the last year?"

"I didn't break them. And I'm the rough one? You're the one who dropped your cell phone in the pool last summer!"

Her mouth dropped. "You pushed me in!" She was fuming. "And maybe next time you skateboard you should carry your own stuff!" She stormed toward the car. He followed, carrying his board beneath his left arm.

The car ride was quiet. The only noise was Jeremy mindlessly humming the jingle to that annoying ravioli commercial on TV. Singing that ravioli jingle had sort of become tradition among their circle of friends every time they were in her car. Jeremy had started it. He was the first to call her hand-me-down Rav4 the Ravioli. Then, ever since the ravioli commercial had come out with the pseudo-family sitting around a table while the mom dished up ravioli from a can, they'd begun singing the jingle every time they got in her car. At the time it was funny, but at the moment she wished he would hum himself to sleep. She flipped on the radio and Kanye and Estelle burst from the speakers. Even though she wasn't really in the mood for one of her favorite songs, "American Boy," it was still better than listening to him hum.

She'd dated Jeremy for nearly two years, and the first year had been wonderful. She'd been so nervous and excited every time he came around. The butterflies she'd felt were unlike anything she'd ever experienced in her life. Even getting up for school in the morning had suddenly seemed exciting. What had made life so wonderful was that she would see him. He'd wait for her next to her locker. Every time he reached for her hand and held it as they walked across campus, she'd felt her heart race. Not to seem like a dork, but she truly understood what it felt like to be giddy. She'd been so nervous about her first kiss and even holding his hand that she'd lost sleep and had stomachaches. What if he'd thought she was a bad kisser or her hands were extra sweaty from nerves when they held hands? But he'd been so sweet and patient that eventually the first kiss had come naturally. Then cuddling up to him while watching a movie was as simple as breathing. She felt so comfortable around him. However, the comfort turned to something different.

Little by little, she got tired of sitting around while he played his Nintendo Wii for three hours straight, listening to *his* favorite music blast from his iPod speakers. She didn't even like most of his music. He liked all this death rocker music with singers who sounded like they were constantly screaming. She liked singers who actually sounded like they had talent, like Alicia Keys and Jack White.

Every single person she knew would wonder how on earth she'd become bored with

Jeremy Maddox. *The* Jeremy Maddox. Not only was he unarguably one of the cutest guys on campus, but he was popular and funny and good at everything he did, which was just about anything. What was wrong with her? In the spring he was the star pitcher for the Coyotes baseball team. In the summer he competed in surf competitions and won. And then in the winter he snowboarded down triple-diamond mountains. Not to mention his charming personality, which had won over all her friends and family.

Her doubt about their relationship had started with a snowboarding trip earlier this year. They'd made the trek up to Big Bear. Natalie had hoped Jo would join them, but she had to work that morning at the bookstore. Matt was supposed to go too, but had flaked at the last minute with the flu.

It had just been Natalie and Jeremy, which was rare. It seemed like they'd always had a group of friends with them everywhere they went. Matt was practically a fixture in their lives, and then there were all Jeremy's baseball teammates and his surfing and skating buddies.

Natalie had only been skiing a few times in her life, and after a couple hours on the slopes she'd decided she'd be okay if she never went skiing or snowboarding again. She was a warm weather person. She couldn't understand the point of putting on her body weight in puffy, uncomfortable clothes and heavy, rigid boots, waiting in line for an eternity at a ski lift only to ride with a freezing face up a mountain and soar back down within ten seconds. The thrill was not worth the work. Not to mention that after one of her ten million slips on the snow, a chunk of ice had managed to sneak up her hat and freeze her ear like a popsicle. The strangest part was that her ear didn't even feel numb. It had gotten so cold that it burned. Her ear had turned all red and chunky in places.

"You have frostbite," a motherly woman in the ski lift line had informed her.

The only thing she had known of frostbite was from a made-for-TV movie about a couple with a baby who were trapped in the snow for days on end, living out of their freezing car with a dead battery and eating ice while begging God for searchers to find them. In the end, they were rescued and taken to a hospital, where their black frostbitten feet were amputated. So she'd sat by herself in the ski lodge looking in the mirror every ten minutes to see if her ear was turning black. Jeremy had left her to snowboard and, honestly, hadn't seemed all that concerned about her ear.

As she sat by herself in the ski lodge, she couldn't help but wonder if Jeremy would still love her if she had only one ear. It would be pretty easy to conceal the flaw with her hair and everything, but would Jeremy be able to overlook this freakish quirk? She figured he'd be able to live with it, but there was still a tiny part of her that just didn't know how he would react.

Ever since that day the wheels had been turning in her mind. Maybe he wasn't the right guy for her. She took it as a bad sign that she even had to ask herself if he would care if she had one ear. How could she even think that he wouldn't care? Wouldn't you automatically know your boyfriend would still love you if you had only one ear? It shouldn't even be a question, right? Maybe they always had so much fun together because they were with all their favorite people—all their friends. But when left alone they really weren't right for each other. She'd debated asking him for a break—just some time apart from each other so they could figure things out. But then his parents had separated. The change had been hard on him, and in his own Jeremy way he'd confided in her. It hadn't been like he spilled his guts with tears and everything. He was a guy, after all. But he seemed like he really needed her.

She pulled up in front of his house. Instead of getting out of the car, he sat for a moment. "Look, I'm sorry I snapped at you about my shades."

"It's okay," she said, even though she sort of felt like reiterating that she hadn't broken his shades to begin with. But at that point she was hungry and had homework and didn't really feel like arguing again over who broken his shades.

"Well, I don't want us to say good-bye and be mad at each other." He leaned in and pecked her on the lips. It was a quick kiss and his lips felt soft. "You want to go to the movies tomorrow night?" he asked.

She shrugged. "Sure. Let me just see how homework goes."

"All right."

They said good-bye. After he closed the door, she glanced in her rearview mirror. The flower he'd given her lay crunched beneath her purse.

Three

After she'd come home from dropping off Jeremy, she was pleasantly surprised to find that her little brother Thomas had finally fixed whatever technical issue that had caused her computer to completely wig out for the past few days. He'd attempted to explain in detail what had gone wrong, and she found herself more excited by Jeremy's new skateboard. As he rambled on about hard drives and other words that sounded like they belonged on spaceships, she zoned out.

She gave Thomas a brotherly pat on the back. "Thanks. You saved my life. Now go get me a Diet Coke and the bag of Doritos."

"Brandon ate all the Doritos again, and Grandma Jones had the last Diet Coke."

Figured. There was never enough food in the house with two boys and her grandmother, who ate out of boredom.

"All right, a glass of water and one of those protein bars that Mom eats." She assumed they were the only things left in the house to snack on because they tasted like cardboard, and no one except her mother ever touched them.

He quickly scurried away.

Thomas was the good twin. He helped with the occasional computer repair and often went for snacks. Probably the only things her brothers had in common were that they were both twelve and idolized Jeremy. Natalie often felt so much older and different from them. Thomas, the computer geek, spent most of his afternoons inventing things. Brandon, the rebel of the family, spent most of his time trying to figure out how to blow up Thomas's inventions. They were both completely banned from Natalie's room and bathroom unless Thomas was fixing her computer or figuring out a way for her nail polish to dry faster.

She spent the remainder of her time before dinner working on her column. The whole dog-costume-in-the-newsroom ordeal had set her back.

She'd barely finished a rough first draft of the column when her mother's voice reverberated from every corner of the house.

"Dinner!"

Natalie often wondered how her mother had managed to keep her vocal cords intact with all her dinner yelling every night.

"Everyone wash hands!"

Downstairs Natalie found her family standing around two large boxes of Round Table pizza. *Yes!* Pizza night was always welcome.

"Grab yourself a drink," her mother said before she handed Natalie a paper plate. Ever since her mother had taken a part-time job teaching sociology at the local community college, her family had enjoyed several pizza nights. Her mother passed out paper plates before everyone gathered around the kitchen table.

"What is this on my pizza?" Grandma Jones asked. She scrutinized the display of ham, green onions, pineapple, and bacon that covered the cheese.

"It's dog barf," Brandon said.

Her father shot him a look. "Brandon,

not at the table." Her father was fresh from work also. He worked for a home loan company, and his job had taken quite a hit with the economy and real estate doing so badly in California. So last year her parents had made the decision for Mom to go back to work and Grandma Jones to move out here to "help" with the kids. Natalie didn't really think they needed help. Her brothers were twelve. She was sixteen. It wasn't like they needed a babysitter. Not to mention Grandma had no control over the boys and spent most of her hours watching *Nancy Grace* and movies on Lifetime.

The only one who needed help was Grandma Jones. She was always hitting up Natalie for rides to T.J. Maxx and Dollar Tree.

"This is a Hawaiian-style pizza, Grandma," Natalie said.

"Well, if I wanted a Hawaiian pizza, I would've gone to Hawaii. Whatever happened to the basics? Some good pepperoni. Maybe some black olives." Grandma Jones had tried to dye her hair last week, and it had turned out sort of blue. She didn't seem to mind, though, or maybe she didn't even notice. Natalie wasn't sure. No bigger than

40

Natalie's little brothers, Grandma Jones made up for her small size in personality. Her opinions were large and loud. Everything Grandma Jones did spoke in volumes. She wore loud colors, painted her nails red, and gossiped without whispering.

It was sort of interesting to listen to Grandma Jones talk about the neighbors and about Natalie's uncle with four divorces and a bad gambling habit. Grandma Jones always kept it real—there was no pretending with her. But it drove Natalie's mother insane.

They spent the remainder of dinner listening to her brothers belch and Grandma Jones tell stories of the days when there was better, more practical pizza available. Natalie stuffed herself with pizza and soda before returning to her room.

She spent another hour working on the column before deciding it was the best she could do. A bad feeling had been haunting her ever since she'd returned home, and not because of her fight with Jeremy or her dislike of the newspaper column. It was the same feeling that haunted her when she ran out the front door late for school and wondered if she had left her straightening iron on.

She figured she just needed a visit to Romeohelpme. The website was the only place she could share her true feelings about love and relationships. Romeohelpme was an advice website where teens could post questions about love and then their peers posted replies on a message board. There was a FAQ section with common questions like "How do I ask a girl to a dance?"— questions like the ones Natalie got for her column. She'd never been able to find any of her own personal questions in the FAQ section, but she'd made a few loyal cyber friends by posting her curious questions about love and relationships.

She looked at the disk with her latest column sitting next to her computer and couldn't believe the fact that the "expert" behind Coyote Courtship was a regular on Romeohelpme. She felt like a character on one of Grandma Jones's Lifetime movies. Soccer mom by day, stripper by night. It was a double life.

In the column she'd written everything everyone wanted to hear. She thought about the latest piece she'd written about the dance. *Now is not the time to worry about dropping subtle hints. If the guy you want to ask to the dance sits next to you in one of your classes, don't be shy. Maybe he's hoping you'll ask. Or if the girl you want to ask you hasn't made a move, let her know you're available. If you let fear get in the way, you may be missing the biggest opportunity of your life—your biggest shot at love.* She couldn't believe they were her own words. She felt like such a hypocrite. Why? Because fear would always get in the way of her love life. But was it fear or obligation? And how had she ended up with all these crazy feelings? Most of these feelings she couldn't even share with Jo. Really, the message board on Romeohelpme was her only outlet. She had to ask the world.

She called herself Up All Night, and the only information she ever shared about herself was that she was female. The website was made for teens, but these days everyone had to be careful of cyber creeps.

Would you still love me if I had one ear?
Member: Up All Night
Advanced Member

    I once had frostbite, and for a moment
I wondered if I was going to have to
have my ear amputated. I know, I know,
it's a bit of a stretch. But for a girl from

California it seemed feasible considering my ear turned the color of tomato soup and burned so badly I almost thought I wanted it removed. Why, you're asking, am I writing about frostbite? Well, I guess it's because on that frostbitten day a big question hit me, and ever since I haven't been able to shake it from my thoughts. Would my boyfriend still love me if I had one ear? I mean, if you really thought you'd found the right person, wouldn't you automatically know the answer? When I read *Romeo and Juliet* last year in lit, I knew that Juliet would never wonder if Romeo would still love her. Or take my parents; I mean, God knows they bicker over everything, but I guarantee you they both know that if one of them lost an ear they would still be in it for the long haul. So shouldn't I know the answer to this question? If you've found the right person, is it ever a question? Or maybe not. Maybe it really takes time to find out the answer. What do you think?

She logged off and decided to begin her nightly ritual of taking a shower before

Grandma Jones invaded the bathroom they now shared. It would give her some time to wait for posts to come in on Romeohelpme. After she finished, she spent a good hour with her hair dryer and flat iron. Everyone always marveled over Natalie's perfect black bob, but the truth was she'd never be able to make it as precise and sharp as she did without her flat iron. The iron had been a birthday gift a couple years back, and it hadn't been cheap. Her mom had special-ordered it from her hairdresser. But it was one of her favorite possessions. After she was finished with her hair, she sat in her bathrobe in front of her computer.

Her heart always skipped a beat when she realized that people had replied to her posts. Sometimes she'd get ten replies. She loved the conversation between her peers, even if she had no idea who any of them were.

Member: Glamour Girl
Advanced Member
RE: Would you still love me if I had one ear?
    OMG! We are so in the same boat. I don't know the answer. Maybe it takes time. Curious to see what everyone else says.

Member: Dragon Guy
Advanced Member
RE: Would you still love me if I had one ear?
Frostbite sucks. I wonder how they would remove your ear and what they would do with it after. I bet you could get a fake one and maybe your boyfriend would never know.

Interesting, she hadn't thought about a fake ear. Nowadays, prosthetics probably came in all varieties. Even though a fake ear wasn't the point, Natalie still saw some symbolism there. If she had to get a fake ear to make her boyfriend love her, would that mean their whole relationship was a facade?

It was the next response that was the most interesting.

Member: Ralph London
Newbie
RE: Would you still love me if I had one ear?
If you have to ask, I think you already know the answer.

Natalie knew deep down what Ralph London meant. And she knew that whoever

Ralph London was, he was probably right. She looked at the name Ralph London and wondered where her cyber friend had come up with the code name. Were they references to something? Or was it like the pen name thing, where you take your middle name and combine it with the first street you lived on? Like, for instance, if she were to take a pen name, she would be Frances Rockhurst because her middle name was Frances and the first house she ever lived in was on Rockhurst Street. But she hated her middle name, and she wasn't about to give any details about herself that could reveal her identity on this website.

She caught a whiff of something bad and instantly recognized the scent of Prints William. Why her grandmother's dog had formed an obsession with Natalie's room was a mystery. She looked under her bed skirt and, sure enough, there he was, his underbite prominent beneath his glassy eyes.

"Prints William, what are you doing? C'mon. Get out of there."

Sometimes she felt kind of sorry for him. He was so ugly, and he had to hide from Taffy, the family cat. Taffy was totally capable of kicking Prints William's butt.

Natalie felt torn between love and hate for the dog. When her grandmother had first come to live with them last year, Natalie had been excited that they were going to have a dog. Prints William was a friendly but strange-looking little dachshund with his terrible teeth and protruding belly. But his rancid breath and overall dog stench had sort of changed her feelings about him. His breath alone could wilt a palm tree.

What made it worse was that her grandmother took the dog everywhere with her—even the doctor's office. Natalie's parents were always getting into fights over Prints William because Natalie's mom didn't think it was a big deal that Grandma Jones took the dog to church and the mall, while Natalie's father couldn't stand it. Really, Natalie thought there was much more behind their Prints William argument, and the dog might just be a scapegoat for all her father's pent-up tension over having Grandma Jones move in with them in the first place. Ever since Natalie had heard the term "scapegoat," she'd liked using it. It meant that an easy target was blamed for something more significant. Jeremy had first mentioned the term after telling Natalie about the family counseling he had to attend after his parents had decided to separate.

Natalie wished she could say her grandmother was cool enough to name her dog after the hottest royal in the world. But Grandma Jones had picked up the dog at the animal shelter near her retirement community eight years ago, and that was the name he'd come with. Apparently, the clever little Prints part of it was that he'd been leaving paw prints all over his kennel. The dog resembled nothing of the real Prince William.

Out of pity, Natalie almost decided to endure the dog's fish-breath odor a little longer. But when she heard her grandmother quietly calling for him, she thought it best to send the dog back to Grandma Jones, who had apparently lost her sense of smell sometime within the last decade.

She couldn't sleep and decided to text Jo. Even though she knew her alarm would feel like an electrocution in about six short hours, she craved a "Night-Light Chat." That's what they called their late-night conversations.

U still up?

She propped herself on a pillow while she waited to hear from Jo.

Her eyes started to feel heavy, and just as she thought Jo had probably retired for the evening, her cell phone rang. It was Jeremy.

"You awake?" he asked. He never called her this late unless something was on his mind. But ever since his parents had split up, he'd chatted on the phone more. He'd never been the type to plunge too deep into his feelings. He barely scratched the surface with Natalie when discussing his troubles. She figured he called just because he was feeling a little lonely and probably insecure. A lot had changed in his life, and maybe Natalie was the only steady thing he had to rely on. The whole frostbite thing had raised a lot of questions about his commitment, and he'd seemed like he wanted to do more things with his friends—without her. Now suddenly she had become like a light in the darkness for him.

"Yeah, I'm still up." She rolled over in bed and flipped off her light. She liked to chat in the dark. "What are you doing?" she asked. Usually he was glued to his Wii by this point in the evening.

"I'm just hanging on my balcony." What he referred to as his balcony was more of a large window ledge that was probably never intended for more than decoration. He'd popped out his screen a long time ago and had sat out there looking at stars and just hanging out when he needed some alone time. "What about you? What have you been up to all evening?"

Oh, just corresponding with complete strangers about whether or not you would still be my boyfriend if I had one ear. "Just the usual. Dinner with the fam. Homework. You know."

"My dad has a girlfriend." His voice sounded heavy.

The remark took Natalie by surprise. "Oh . . . are you sure?"

"Yeah, he told me over the phone. I guess he's been seeing her for a couple weeks now. He wants Chad and me to meet her next weekend."

"I thought he was in counseling with your mom."

"I did too."

"I'm sorry, Jere. Are you okay?"

"I'm fine." He answered a little too quickly. "I mean, I guess I just don't know what to think. I knew things weren't going well, and honestly I thought it would be kind of cool having them separated. They wouldn't both be around breathing down my neck all the time. But now it's just a hassle. And my mom is all bummed out. I hate seeing my mom so sad. It sucks."

She suspected he'd never opened up like this to anyone—even Matt. She remembered the day Jeremy's parents had separated. He'd even gotten choked up when he'd told her. All she could really do was listen. She'd known he wasn't looking for a bunch of crapola love-column Dr. Phil–type advice. He'd just needed to tell someone. It was the same now.

The other end of the phone was so quiet that she could hear coyotes howling by his house. They sounded echoic and faint. She didn't know what to say. "I think you just need to think about yourself for now, Jere. Don't worry about everything so much, you know? Let your parents figure it out. Just be you. Maybe your dad just needs to figure things out. Maybe he just needs some time." As she said the words she felt like such a jerk, because she could sort of relate to his dad.

"I guess." He didn't sound optimistic. "Nat, sometimes I think you're the only real person I have in the world. You and Matt."

She knew that whatever happened she

could not take time for herself at this point. In spite of the fact that she had doubts about their romantic relationship, she still cared deeply for him as a friend. She didn't think she could stand to see him suffer anymore. "You know I'm always here for you."

"Promise."

"Of course."

He was quiet again, and then he seemed to snap out of his funk. His voice picked up a beat. "So we have to start hunting for our costumes."

"That's right." She was happy for his change of mood.

They chatted for a few more minutes before saying good night. She pulled her blankets up around her shoulders and thought of all her mixed feelings. She tried to think if she knew of anyone who'd been in a similar situation to her love life. Only the movies—specifically tragedies.

She could hear coyotes howling outside. They often cried in the night. The bad feeling came over her again. As she turned over in bed it hit her like a ton of bricks. She'd never closed out the computer screen in the newsroom. She had left the newsroom in such a haste she'd forgotten that she'd only hit minimize. She'd never actually closed it out. That meant that anyone could walk in and read what she had written. No one knew she was behind the column except Matt, who was one of the last people she wanted to see it. What if he told Jeremy?

Four

The only other time Natalie had woken up before her alarm clock had been when she'd first begun dating Jeremy. Her excitement level back then had been so intense that she'd naturally risen with the sun. Butterflies had squashed her appetite. Rather than eating breakfast she'd spend an hour on hair and makeup.

On this particular morning her eyes popped open before the sound of her alarm clock greeted her. She skipped breakfast, and she couldn't help but think of the irony. Once, she'd gotten up early for love, and now she was getting up early to avoid having anyone discover that she was so con-flicted by love. She'd been up half the night worrying. She was *pretty* sure that Matt wouldn't tell Jeremy about the column and all her bleak opinions about relationships. Guys didn't run and tell each other stuff like that, and Matt was just cool that way. He wasn't nosy and certainly wasn't the type to stir up drama. But the risk was still there. Besides, she didn't want Matt to know her true feelings either. Her sarcasm had really been for her own entertainment, and thinking of Matt reading her silly words was embarrassing.

Parking on campus a half hour before school started was the only bonus she could find from the whole situation. Most mornings she ended up in the Outer Space parking lot. She ran to the English building, which housed the journalism room. While sprinting across campus, she realized there was a good chance she'd have to wait for Mr. Moore, the newspaper adviser, to arrive so he could unlock the door. Oh Lord, what if he didn't arrive until right before classes began, or worse, later in the day? She'd never come to the newsroom this early. For all she knew it was closed until third period, which meant she'd either get detention or have to wait to fix her little problem.

She felt a mixture of relief and terror when she noticed that the newsroom door was propped open. Relief that she'd be able to get in there, and terror her true feelings had already been exposed.

When she entered, Matt was seated at the same computer she'd been sitting at yesterday. *No!* Maybe there was a small chance he hadn't seen her little minimized article in the bottom corner, or maybe he'd just figured that since it wasn't his own work he should just leave it untouched.

"Hey, Natalie," he said. His light blue eyes were almost the same exact color as his T-shirt. She couldn't help it if she thought he was cute. He wasn't the kind of guy that was drop-dead gorgeous—like Jeremy—but there was something about him. His blond shaggy curls, his dimples, and his long eyelashes. He looked sweet, but also strong and capable with his broad shoulders and sinewy arms.

"Matt, you're here early." She tried to act casual, as though her early arrival was routine.

"So are you. Your computer still down?"

"No. Actually, I just came to give you my latest column." She tried not to make it obvious as she glanced at the screen. Her work was gone.

He seemed surprised. "Natalie? The biggest procrastinator at the paper is handing in her article early?" Anyone acquainted with Natalie knew that getting things done early was so not her style. She was more the "come screeching in at the last minute" type of girl—with everything.

"Well, you know. I just wanted to get it over with."

"Mr. Moore will be stoked too. That's cool that you're enjoying the column."

If he only knew. Obviously, he hadn't seen the phony column.

He sighed. "We are so swamped."

It was no secret that the paper was slammed whenever there was a big event like a theme dance on campus. "Is there anything else I can do to help?" she asked.

He thought for a moment. "How do you feel about picking up an extra feature article? I'm sure Mr. Moore will give you extra credit for it, and I've already done some of the work. I could fill you in after school today. We could do it together."

Natalie had mentioned to Jo that she might swing by after school today, and she was actually feeling really good about having all of her assignments behind her, but how could she say no? He seemed like he really needed the help. "Yeah, all right. What's it about?"

"Finding just the right Halloween costume. I talked about it with Mr. Moore, and we're hoping for some creative ideas—fresh things that no one has ever come as before. And I thought it might be cool to add, like, a Halloween costume quiz at the end. Something like 'What does your costume really say about you?' or 'What costume best suits your personality?'"

"I love it! That sounds like fun." Natalie loved personality quizzes and was always taking them in all her favorite magazines. The newspaper had never done anything like this before.

"You want to meet back here after last period?" she asked.

He nodded.

If he'd seen the other column, he certainly wasn't acting like it, but then that meant someone else had probably seen it and closed out the screen. But they wouldn't know who she was, anyway. She fished around in her backpack for the disk, and when she glanced up she realized that all the other computers in the room were turned off. She pulled out the disk and sat at a computer next to Matt. "So these computers get turned off every night?" she asked.

"Yes. The custodian, I'm pretty sure, shuts everything down. All I know is that whenever I come back in the morning they're turned off."

Hallelujah! It sounded like the only person who could've potentially seen the fake column was the janitor. And what would he care?

It was halfway through lunchtime before she finally ran into Jo. Her best friend came toward her with a look of mischief in her eyes—not an uncommon look for Jo. Her black hair was pulled into a ponytail at the nape of her neck. She was dressed in an expensive-looking pair of skinny jeans with a silver tank top. A stylish pair of pointy flats with little buckles over the tips completed the look. Jo always looked good in clothes. She rarely came to school in an outfit that didn't attract compliments. Natalie, on the other hand, dressed for comfort. Converse All Stars, her favorite destroyed jeans, tank tops, and hooded sweatshirts made up her uniform.

Jo was also one of those lucky girls who never had to worry about a tan. Her Iranian heritage had given her the bonus of beautiful bronzed skin, exotic features, and a grandmother who could tell fortunes. Natalie's skin was the color of a baby's butt, and her grandmother came with Prints William.

Jo's angelic face featured big round dark eyes that always seemed to appear inquisitive and caring. "So, can you keep a huge secret?" Jo asked.

Whenever anyone phrased a question with those words, the answer was yes. Who in their right mind would say no when it sounded like juicy news was on the way? "Of course. You didn't think I'd say no, did you?"

"So, I just came from the Howl at the Moon committee meeting, and guess who is on the ballot for the couples costume queen and king for the second year in a row?"

Natalie knew the answer, but for some reason didn't want to admit it. "Who?"

"You!" Her eyes widened as she pointed to Natalie. "You and Jeremy!"

"Oh. Great!"

"Oh great?"

"Well, you know how I've been feeling."

"I know, but it's just the school dance. It will be fun." Jo knew how Natalie felt, but Natalie sensed that she didn't fully understand. It was like Jo just thought that Natalie was going through a phase.

"Have you figured out who you're going to ask yet?" Natalie asked. It was a sore subject, mostly because the guy Jo had a crush on had already been asked. Poor Jo had been waiting all summer for this dance, finally working up the nerve to ask Brian Gonzalez. As soon as Howl at the Moon bids went on sale, Kelly Green may as well have been riding a broomstick when she swept in and asked Brian before Jo had a chance.

She shrugged. "I'm not sure. I'm never going to find anyone at this stupid school. I'll be single the rest of my life." Jo was always doom and gloom when it came to her love life, mostly because she'd never had a boyfriend. She was dying for one. It was often hard for Natalie to complain about her own love life when Jo thought Natalie was the luckiest person on earth.

"You can always take Vincent."

Jo sighed. "I know. But for once I'd

like to go to the dance with someone where sparks actually fly." She changed the subject, as she always did when Natalie tried to bring up any romantic possibilities between Jo and Vincent. "Are you coming over today?" Jo asked.

"I think I'm going to be a little late. I promised Matt I would meet him in the newsroom. I guess there's a lot of work for the Halloween issue of the paper, and I said I would help with another article."

"Try to swing by after that. Seto said she would read our cups."

Natalie felt a surge of excitement. Jo's grandmother, Seto, could see the future by reading the inside of teacups. It was the coolest thing ever, and Natalie would never pass up an opportunity to have her fortune told, especially at a time when she needed so much guidance. "I'm there." As she waved good-bye to Jo, she felt a knot in her stomach. She was excited to have her cups read, but the future seemed so uncertain.

Five

Mr. Moore greeted Natalie when she entered the newsroom. A few of her fellow staff writers also waved.

"So, you're going to take on our personality quiz," Mr. Moore said.

Natalie nodded. "It sounds like fun."

"Good. I think you're just the right person for that assignment." He'd said that about the love column too. And now look.

Mr. Moore couldn't be nicer. Always encouraging and enthusiastic, he was a well-liked teacher on campus. But sometimes it was hard to overlook how nerdy he was. He always carried pencils in the front pocket of his short-sleeved button-down plain white shirts. He practically devoured boring magazines and had once confessed that he read a nonfiction book a week. He even read some of his favorites twice. His square glasses were tight around his temples, and his shoes looked like they were either expensive orthopedics or very cheap ugly black shoes with soles like tires that he'd found at a discount store.

Matt looked as though he'd never left the newsroom. He was seated at the same computer and still looked busy. He ran his fingers through his hair before turning to face Natalie.

"I'm starving," he said. "You want to hit up Denny's while we figure this out?"

"Sure." She was hungry too, and getting away from campus was always a good thing. They said good-bye to Mr. Moore and some of their classmates before heading to the parking lot.

They rode in his car. She noticed traces of beach sand on the seats and the floor of his old pickup truck, evidence that he'd been surfing in his free time. The truck smelled faintly of sunscreen and surf wax. They lived a good forty minutes from the beach, but Matt was always escaping to the coast whenever he could. Natalie had seen him surf on many trips to the beach with Jeremy. Matt was a good surfer—graceful on the water. Unlike Jeremy, Matt surfed for fun. Jeremy was always so competitive about everything. If he was good at anything, he wanted to be in competitions. He wanted to be the best.

They drove across town to Denny's. Natalie loved this time of day. She'd never been a morning person. School was out. The afternoon sun cast shadows over the trees in Oak Canyon. Oak Canyon had every kind of tree one could think of. Maybe it was because they lived in southern California and all kinds of trees could thrive in the warm weather. Of course, oak trees with their little boatlike leaves covered most of the terrain. But there were palm trees and pine trees too. Orange trees and millions of avocado trees.

"I had a chance to read the column," Matt said.

"That was fast."

"Good work." Matt flipped on his blinker as they turned down Canyon Boulevard. "I think it will answer a lot of questions for people—make it easier to find dates."

"I hope so."

Matt had originally talked her into taking the column. She could still remember his exact words when he'd approached her: "You're the perfect candidate for this," he'd said. "You and Jeremy are the real deal. What better person to write about love?"

It was starting to feel hot in the car, so Natalie rolled down her window.

"So are you doing anything for Jeremy's birthday this year?" Matt asked as he rolled down his window too. "The party you threw last year was great."

Natalie hadn't forgotten that Jeremy's birthday was a week before Halloween. He'd be seventeen. She knew he'd probably be expecting another big party. Last year she'd orchestrated a beach bonfire party. She remembered cuddling up next to him while they'd toasted marshmallows with all his friends. She remembered how warm she'd felt in his arms, how things had been so comfortable between them. "I'll probably organize another party. I'm not sure where yet."

"Bowling would be fun," Matt suggested.

"Bowling? I hadn't even thought of bowling." This was probably due to the fact that she didn't have an athletic bone in her body. She liked to watch sports, and that was about it. But bowling could be fun. It wasn't like she had to tackle, kick, or run after any-thing. "That's not a bad idea."

"They have rock-and-bowl at the bowl-ing alley on Friday nights. The radio station broadcasts there, and they play good music the whole time you bowl."

"Jeremy would probably love that. I'll invite all his friends."

"I can help with anything," Matt offered.

"Thanks."

They chatted about the paper and the other articles that students were working on. "You going to the dance?" Natalie asked.

"No date yet."

"You? No date?" Did she sound like she was flirting? Because she hadn't meant to sound like she was flirting. "I mean . . . what I mean was that I just thought this would be something you wouldn't want to miss out on. I mean, this is our junior year and we only have two more Howl at the Moons left."

She didn't even sound like herself. Why did she feel so uncomfortable? She tried to squash all her funny feelings by encouraging Matt to find a date. "Any ideas about who you would like to go with?" she asked.

He seemed as though he were squirming a little at the question.

"You do! You totally have a crush on someone." She was curious.

He smiled and shook his head. "No, I don't."

"Why don't you have a girlfriend, Matt?"

His smile faded slightly and he shrugged. "I don't know. Guess I just haven't found the right girl. Not everyone is as lucky as Jeremy and you." They were at a stoplight and he turned to look at her for a moment. He looked at her in that way that made her feel as though he had nothing else in the world to look at or think about. *This is just the way Matt is,* she told herself. *This is the way he looks at everyone.*

"We're here." The sound of Matt's voice was distant at first. "Natalie?"

"Uh-huh." She snapped out of her daze. "I mean, yes. Oh, we're here." She reached for her seat belt.

"I thought I'd lost you for a minute there. What are you thinking about?"

"Oh, just school and the article," she answered quickly.

He nodded. "Good. We need lots of ideas for this."

They waited for a hostess to lead them to a booth. Natalie didn't need to look at the menu to know she wanted a large basket of cheese fries with a side of ranch, and a Diet Coke.

Matt scanned the menu for a couple seconds, then set it down. "I think I just want cheese fries."

"That's what I'm getting. You want to just split a huge basket? Maybe get some mozzarella sticks too?" she suggested.

"Sounds good to me."

Matt pulled a folder out of his backpack and placed it on the table. "So, here is what I've started. I made a copy for you." He slid a couple sheets of paper across the table.

It was mostly just couples costume ideas jotted down, and some ideas for the quiz. She scanned them. *Couples from around the world, couples from different time eras, movie theme couples, sports couples . . .*

"What if people want to go with their friends to the dance?" she asked, and then realized this was so something she would ask in her current state of mind. "I mean, you know that every year a group of girls and guys go together with no specific dates.

"True. I thought about that. We'll have to come up with some singles ideas too."

They began to brainstorm—bouncing all

kinds of ideas off each other—pausing only when their food arrived. "For the couples around the world idea a samurai and a geisha would be pretty cool," Matt said.

"Love it." Natalie added it to the list. "And for America we could put Uncle Sam and Betsy Ross or just dressing in all red, white, and blue."

"Great idea."

"And for different time eras we could date all the way back to the prehistoric era with cavemen. Oh! And even Pilgrims. Then there could be the whole Southern belle theme and the gangsters and flappers for the twenties." She dipped a fry in ranch dressing, and Matt picked up her thoughts where she left off.

"Then the fifties, and the hippies in the sixties. Yeah, I mean, the list goes on and on."

"I have the best idea. We could even put an opposites category in there. Like, someone could go as 'the past' and go as a caveman and someone could go as 'the future' and go as a robot."

Matt loved the opposites idea. "How about hot and cold? One person could come in full beach attire and the other could come in a ski suit. People wouldn't even need to buy a costume for that. All you'd need is a bathing suit and a snowboarding outfit."

"Maybe we should do an affordable costume column too. Where people could just find the simplest things in their house to make a costume from. I once read a book where the character went as white trash, and all she put on was a white trash bag. She just cut holes for the arms and the head."

Matt tossed his head back and laughed. "That is hilarious!"

They had fun brainstorming costume ideas, and Natalie couldn't believe how easy it was to come up with things when she had a creative partner. They decided they would give only a few specific costume ideas for each general theme. The article was meant to inspire people to come up with their own ideas, and to have as much fun as Natalie and Matt were having while coming up with ideas.

They still hadn't even discussed the quiz when they polished off the last cheese fry and mozzarella stick. With the two of them working together, the article would be a breeze.

"I'm gonna head to the boys' room," Matt said, excusing himself.

It was a couple seconds after he left when

Natalie realized she felt a little surge of irritation in her mouth—specifically in the upper front teeth region. Alarm hit when she sensed the familiar feeling of something stuck in her tooth. She'd had something stuck between her teeth this whole time? She ran her tongue over the spot, and sure enough, it detected something hard and foreign. What was it? An herb from the mozzarella stick crust? Or had it been there since her granola bar and Doritos binge at lunch? She wanted to die. What she needed to do was run to the bathroom. However, all of their stuff was on the table, including Matt's wallet and backpack. She picked up a spoon from the table, and tried to examine her mouth in the reflection. But the spoon was too tarnished. She ran her finger over the spot, but whatever was in there was stubborn. She lifted her front lip and snarled in the window next to her. Maybe she could see from her reflection. But she could only see the outline of her head.

This was horrible. She reached for her glass and began to swish Diet Coke vigorously between her cheeks as though it were mouthwash. She was midswish and looking chipmunklike when Matt appeared out of nowhere. She spit her Diet Coke back into the glass.

"You all right?" he asked.

She didn't want to open her mouth too wide and expose whatever was lodged between her two front teeth. "I'm fine," she said between gritted teeth. Her voice sounded funny through her clenched teeth.

"Did you see someone outside? Someone from school?" he asked as he slid back into the booth.

She shook her head this time.

"I thought I saw you smiling at someone outside."

"It was just a dog." She was still speaking through her gritted teeth. She sounded like she was underwater.

"You sure you're all right?"

She jumped up. "Will you excuse me for a minute?"

She didn't wait for his answer. She scurried to the bathroom and quickly removed what appeared to be mozzarella stick crust. She decided this might go down as the most embarrassing moment of her life. She'd rather wear the Dalmatian suit to prom. How long had he been staring at fried food residue while she was rambling on about costumes of the world? She wanted to die.

When she returned, he was reading over his notes.

"Everything all right?" he asked.

Natalie smiled big. "Great." *I just want to drive off a cliff, but thank you for acting like you never noticed the food stuck between my teeth.*

He lifted his eyebrows. "All right, then. Back to business."

She was glad he could forget her mozzarella mouth and move on so quickly. This would haunt her until she was senile.

It was hard to focus after that. Natalie was jittery and weird and wished she could just feel normal. If it had been Jo or Vinny, she wouldn't care. Or even Jeremy, for that matter. That's when she admitted it to herself. Sitting there in Denny's, wishing for floss, she realized that she had a crush on Matt. It was more than a little attraction. She felt butterflies, and felt self-conscious, and everything people feel when they're falling for someone. This realization made her feel terrible. What if Jeremy was checking out other girls, or Jo? The truth was, she didn't know. She convinced herself that the only reason she felt this way was because she was confused—period. She wasn't thinking straight. These were crazy-person thoughts. She needed to come to her senses. He was cute. That was it. Who could blame her for feeling a little giddy around him?

She needed to get out of there, quickly.

"Listen, why don't I just do the quiz myself? You have so many other things to deal with at the paper. And I'm not that busy, so I'll do it."

He looked surprised. "Really?" he asked with hesitation in his voice.

"Positive."

"Wow, thanks, Nat. This makes my life easier." He raised his Diet Coke glass. "To more Denny's meetings," he said.

Their glasses clinked. "To more meetings." Her heart skipped a beat.

Six

Natalie made a conscious effort not to tap her foot on the carpet as she waited for Jo's grandmother, Seto, to finish reading her tea-cup. Jo sat next to her on the couch, flipping through an *Us Weekly*, occasionally lifting her head to comment on someone's lack of fashion sense.

"Look at what the Olsen twins are wearing in this picture. Would someone please fire their stylist already?"

Natalie had already taken her turn with the magazine while Seto had read Jo's cup. She glanced at the picture, though. "I know. And they have such cute faces. Why do they dress like that?"

Having Seto read one's cups was the ultimate treat. It wasn't often that Natalie met people who could see the future, and Seto was a master as far as she was concerned. They always had to wait for Seto to offer her services. According to Jo it was rude to ask to have your cups read. When Seto did offer to read their cups, which was once every few months, it was like the best day of the month. They always invited Vincent to join them, but he said he'd rather not know. He said that hearing things in advance might change the way you act and it could affect the future. His thinking made sense to Natalie, but she still couldn't resist peeking ahead. She'd never been one to wait until Christmas Day to see her gifts for the first time. She hated suspense.

Seto and Jo referred to the fortune-telling custom as "reading cups" or "reading tea leaves," but Natalie never saw any leaves in there. After she managed to get the tea down her throat, Seto flipped the cup over, and what looked like mud streaked the inside of the special porcelain cup in veiny little rivulets. The muddy mess inside spelled out Natalie's fortune.

Today, Jo didn't seem happy with her

fortune. Jo always wanted Seto to focus on her love life. When Seto revealed that the cup said there was someone out there for Jo, a smile had flashed across Jo's face. However, when Seto said "but," the smile quickly faded. Seto proceeded to share that Jo wasn't ready for "this someone." It was going to take time. "How much time?" Jo had wanted to know. But Seto had only given the vague answer that it all depended on Jo. Natalie had hoped Seto would be a little more specific when it was her turn.

The tea had tasted like dirt mixed with a strong dose of herbal vitamins. Natalie often thought it would taste like a vitamin if you chewed it. Not to mention the tea was loaded with caffeine and always left the girls wired out of their minds for the remainder of the day.

After she'd taken the last sip of tea, she'd prayed for answers about her complicated love life, her job at the school newspaper, and whether or not her parents would find out that she'd failed a recent geometry test. Then she'd watched Seto, looking for signs of worry. A hard one to read, Seto always examined the mug with her eyebrows slightly raised, occasionally letting out little interested sounds as if she were either pleased by what she saw or totally puzzled. Natalie could never tell. A knot tightened in her stomach, and she understood why Vincent avoided the tradition.

As Natalie waited for Seto to finish, she tried to read her for any clues as to what she saw in there. Would Seto really tell her if disaster was on the horizon? Would she say, "You're going to end up heartbroken and alone for the rest of your life. Scandal is waiting"? It was Seto. She'd practically become a surrogate grandmother to Natalie. Chances were she would sugarcoat the reading a little.

Finally Seto spoke. A native of Iran, she had a thick accent. "This is very good." She pointed a wrinkled finger inside the cup. "You see. You have the lion's head in here. This shows strength. You are very strong. It is a very good sign. You are powerful and you can do anything you vant to do."

Natalie and Jo exchanged excited glances. So far Natalie liked it.

Seto continued. "You have been very vorried lately. You vorry about yourself and other people too. But maybe you think too much. Maybe you think too hard. You know

80

vhat I mean?" She looked up at Natalie.

Natalie nodded.

"You don't need to vorry so much. Let some things go."

Now Seto was starting to sound like her mother. Natalie knew she worried way too much.

"I see a young man in here. No wait, two young men. They care for you and you care for them too. Very much." Natalie felt a chill run up her spine. Two guys? How would Seto know this? There was no way Seto could know how she felt about Matt. She'd only admitted it to herself less than an hour ago, and even if she had known all along, this was so top secret. She wouldn't even let Prints William in on this one.

Seto continued. "It's confusing to you. But don't vorry. Everything vill be fine. One of the boys is a someone who likes you . . . vhat do you call him? A hidden admirer?"

Natalie and Jo chuckled. "You mean a secret admirer, Seto?"

"Yes, secret admirer."

Well, now Natalie knew it couldn't be Matt. He'd always acted as though Jeremy and Natalie were a match made in heaven. He wasn't attracted to Natalie.

"He may give you something you can hold in your hand." Seto sat up and leaned forward as though something important was coming. "Be careful. You try very hard to balance things, but something might be hard to balance. Just be careful."

"What do you mean?"

"Just, you know, vatch what you do." Seto handed the cup to Natalie. "All right, now I vant you to turn the cup upside down and make your vish."

Natalie took the cup and turned it upside down onto the saucer. She thought about what she wanted to wish for. Clarity. Peace of mind. The vision to figure out what she should do with her crazy love life.

Seto looked in the cup, and then at Natalie. "I see you have made your vish, and you vill get him."

Him? Had she subconsciously been wishing for him . . . meaning Matt? She didn't even want to think about the answer.

Natalie noticed Jo raise her eyebrows. "Him?"

Natalie shrugged, then thanked Seto for the reading.

Seto was the coolest grandma, and Jo's whole family was pretty cool too, for that matter. Jo's older sister, Sam, was off at college. Her parents traveled the world constantly, leaving Jo in the care of Seto. Seto was kind and funny, and best of all she went to bed early. Whenever they spent the night, they had Jo's whole mansion to themselves.

Natalie's family life couldn't be more opposite. Her parents never went out of town. Grandma Jones dominated the remote control and snored so loud a neighbor once complained. Her brothers were hooligans. Throw Prints William and the cat into the mix, and it was an insane asylum.

After Seto was finished reading their cups, Jo and Natalie made sundaes and watched a rerun of *My Super Sweet 16* with no interruptions. *Paradise.* Going to Jo's house was like going to a fancy resort—not that Natalie knew what it would be like to go somewhere fancy. But the high ceilings and polished hardwood floors were extravagant. Their front door alone was taller than the first story of Natalie's house, and they had glass cabinets, and frescoes painted over their ceilings. Everything was clean and clutter-free at Jo's. At Natalie's house, fur and her brothers' dirty cleats could always be found on their stained carpet.

"So, announcements for the Howl at the Moon court will come out tomorrow," Jo said.

"I know."

"Don't be so glum. Do you know how many girls would kill to be in your position?"

"I know, but it's just hard to explain. I mean, I still really care about Jeremy, but I'm telling you, I just don't know if he's the right guy for *me*. Sometimes I just think we're kind of opposite. We might be better off just being friends." She thought for a moment. "But then on the other hand, maybe I'd really miss him if I broke up with him."

"Maybe you just need to take a break from him. Just see what it's like without him for a couple weeks. You guys spend so much time together. I bet you'd really miss him."

Natalie shook her head. "I can't take a break from him."

"Why not?" Jo licked the back of her spoon.

"Because it would be so cruel. He's so sad about his parents. I know he doesn't show it a lot to everyone else, but he really is sad. Then with the nominations coming out . . . I feel like I'll be letting him down. It would be such a blow."

Jo's spoon was noisy as she scooped up another bite of ice cream. "I see what you're saying. But maybe you could wait till after the dance. It's only right around the corner. I mean, if you're that torn, it's not fair for you to be unhappy just for someone else's happiness."

"I just don't think I could stand to see him so sad. And to think that it would be my fault." Natalie glanced at the clock. "I should go. I have so much homework." She carried her empty ice cream dish to the kitchen.

"Me too," Jo said. "I have a paper due tomorrow. *The Great Gatsby*," she said, and groaned.

Jo walked Natalie to the driveway.

"Tell Seto thanks again for reading my cups."

"Is there a crush you're not telling me about?" Jo grinned mischievously.

"No." Natalie played it cool. It wasn't a lie. What was the harm in thinking he was cute? And okay, maybe smart and insightful. And creative. And funny.

"I was just thinking again about Seto's

reading. Two guys that you care about? And your wish at the end? Who are you wishing for?"

Natalie smiled. "C'mon, they're just tea-cups. As of right now there is only one guy in my life." She felt weird keeping her secret from her best friend.

"The cups never lie."

Natalie believed her, mostly because before Seto had come to live with Jo's family, Seto had lived in New York and had been bombarded night and day by people seeking truths about the future. Part of the reason Seto had moved was to be with her family, but also to get away from her millions of clients. Jo had told Natalie stories about how Seto had warned people against danger, and when they didn't listen, the danger had come true. Natalie thought about the warning to be careful of juggling too much. Was she talking about the column? Or her love life? Or everything?

What's more important? Loyalty or love?
Member: Up All Night
Advanced Member
    So it's midnight and I have a question for the world. When it comes to love, does

loyalty come first? Are certain people off-limits? For instance, do guys pick their best friends before girls? Or would they pick a girl before their best friend? Just something that's been on my mind lately. Curious as to thoughts on this. All right, if I'm ever going to make it to first period without detention I have to hit the hay. Good night, all.

Even putting that question out there made her feel so shady. She wasn't seriously considering the notion of ever going for Matt. She was curious and not just for herself. She wondered what other people would say or do. It was an interesting and debatable topic. One of the reasons she liked Romeohelpme so much was that she could start conversations with her peers. Maybe she could see things from a different perspective.

Natalie couldn't sleep; she lay in bed listening to Alicia Keys on her iPod and wondering if anyone had replied to her post. Once she put her words out there for everyone to read, it almost became an addiction to see the replies. She loved getting messages. After thirty minutes of tossing and turning, she flipped on her light switch. Then she logged on to the website.

Member: Dragon Guy
Advanced Member
RE: What's more important? Loyalty or love?
    **Bros before hos baby. That's all I have
to say.**

Real nice.

Member: Glamour Girl
Advanced Member
RE: What's more important? Loyalty or love?
    **I think it would depend on the
situation. It would depend on how serious
the relationship was to begin with. If it was
just casual dating then I think it would be
okay, but if it was your boyfriend's best
friend then no—off-limits for sure.**

Several responses followed in the same
vein as Glamour Girl. People agreed—it all
just depended on the situation. The truth
was, Natalie didn't even know the situation. Until his parents had split up, Jeremy
had seemed as though he were drifting
from her a little too. Then all of a sudden
he seemed like he wanted to be closer than
ever.

Member: Skater Chick
Newbie
RE: What's more important? Loyalty or love?
   Dragon Guy, you're an idiot. If you really
like someone in the long run, does it matter?
People should just do whatever they want
and not worry about what everyone else
thinks. Take a look at all the great leaders
and artists. You think they didn't follow their
hearts?

Natalie closed out her computer screen.
Maybe Skater Chick was right. Or maybe
she was wrong. Was it selfish not to care
about what other people thought? She had a
topic for another post.

Seven

"So, Vincent and I are going to the dance together for the third year in a row." Jo swung her dark hair over her shoulders. Natalie sensed the disappointment in her best friend's voice. Though loyal and an awesome friend, Vincent wasn't exactly Jo's idea of a romantic date. It was no secret that he'd had a crush on Jo since they were riding tricycles. However, the feeling wasn't mutual.

"Well, Vincent is always a blast. You know you'll have fun, at least." Natalie had always been cheering for Vincent.

Jo shrugged. "True. Maybe I'll make it to senior prom next year with someone I actually like. I think I'll die boyfriendless." Jo sighed. "Destined to be single forever."

"You know you could have a boyfriend in one second if you wanted one."

"Like who?"

"Like Vinny."

"I love Vincent to death, but just not in that way," Jo said.

Natalie had heard this a million times. She sort of understood why Jo had her reservations about him. He was different from the rest of the guys they hung out with. For example, Vincent was in the drama club and loved musicals. He would gladly go see romantic comedies, and he always had an opinion about the way the girls did their hair. He just seemed to notice more details than most guys they knew. But it was really cool. He just wasn't afraid to be himself. He liked the things he liked, even if they weren't categorized specifically to his gender. Natalie thought it was great. It seemed like girls had so many more options these days. For instance, take Danica Patrick. No one said she was weird because she raced cars. But if you put a guy in a leotard everyone raised their eyebrows. Why were people so weird? Natalie just didn't get it. She was proud of Vincent for being himself.

He wasn't exactly the kind of guy Natalie

pictured slaying dragons to rescue the princess. If he ever wanted to win Jo, he would have to be a dragon slayer. Jo was looking for the fairy-tale love life. But the funny thing was, Vincent was perfect for her and she didn't even see it. They both shared a killer sense of style. Jo's dream was to become a fashion designer or interior decorator. She had a bold slant to her wardrobe and tended to wear things that Natalie would've never had the guts to try on. She was always volunteering for design committees on campus. If there were dances to decorate or homecoming floats to make, she would lead the committee. It was all the same stuff Vincent liked too. They both had a unique appreciation for art.

"He's coming. He's coming . . ." Jo's whisper sounded rushed and nervous.

Natalie knew it was Brian Gonzalez before she even spotted his perfect teeth and deep-set coffee-colored eyes heading their way The whole reason Jo walked with Natalie to fourth period was so Jo could have a "Brian sighting." There was a much faster way for Jo to get to Drawing and Painting. However, once Natalie had informed her that she passed Brian Gonzalez every day in between third and fourth periods, Jo had taken a detour from her Drawing and Painting route and joined Natalie in between classes.

Brian Gonzalez had been Jo's biggest crush since high school had started. She'd even confessed that she'd prayed every single night of the summer for Brian to be in at least one of her classes—except PE—come fall.

He approached quickly. Natalie noticed Jo straighten her back and run her fingers through her hair.

"Hey, Jo." He flicked his chin when he saw her. "What's up?"

"Nothing," she said, producing a nervous smile. The whole encounter lasted less than five seconds, and as soon as he was gone Jo groaned. She turned to Natalie.

"I hate the question 'what's up?'" she said. "I never know what to say. Did he want a whole synopsis of my day, or was I supposed to tell him what I was doing at that exact moment? What do you normally say when people ask you what's up?"

Natalie had never thought about this before. "I don't know. I guess it just depends on the situation. If you called me on the phone and asked me what's up, I would probably give *you* a synopsis of my day. But yeah, I could see how it would be awkward if someone asked you in passing."

"What should I have said? 'Nothing' sounds so boring. I probably sounded like such a dork. I wish I could've said something wonderful and mind-blowing. Did I sound like an idiot?"

"I think he's probably forgotten by now. And I think you answered just fine. I would've said the same thing."

"Really? You swear?"

"Yes. It would've been worse if you had said, 'Oh, just heading to Drawing and Painting to get out my oils and work on the latest still life.'"

Jo cracked up. "True."

"Or what if you had said, 'The only thing that's up is my love for you, Brian. Do you want to go to prom?'"

Jo laughed some more.

They'd come to the fork in their route. Vincent would swoop in at any moment and walk with Jo the rest of the way to Drawing and Painting. His photography class was next door.

"Hey, Vincent," Natalie said.

He had an excited grin on his face. "Guess what?"

"What?" The girls waited for him to answer.

"I just got the lead in *South Pacific*!" His dark eyes lit up.

He looked sharp in his distressed jeans and black-and-purple button-down shirt. He'd left the shirt untucked, and a black straight leather tie completed the look. His mom was a hairdresser at a chic salon downtown and he always had fantastic haircuts. He looked like a rock star. One month he'd be very Pete Wentz, and a few months later he'd be like Brandon Flowers, the lead singer of The Killers.

They took a couple seconds to congratulate their friend before Natalie said goodbye and headed for class.

Just as she was walking away a hand slipped into her own. Before she could even whip around to see its owner, she knew it was Jeremy. They always crossed paths between third and fourth periods. He leaned in and kissed her on the cheek. She caught a whiff of him—his Jeremy scent. She used to love the smell of his shampoo and something else she couldn't define. He'd often left sweatshirts in her car, and she'd wear them to bed at night, smelling his eau de Jeremy. In a way she wanted that excitement back. She wanted to be happy to wear his sweatshirts again. Wouldn't life be far less complicated?

"Second year in a row! Howl at the Moon Court." He gave her a high five with his free hand. Seeing him excited made her happy. "Maybe we'll actually win this time." He smiled at her mischievously. "Jo already told you, didn't she?"

"No way!" She was a terrible liar, and she could tell by the way he laughed that he knew she was lying. "Jo? Tell me? She would never do something like that."

"You girls. You don't keep anything from each other, do you? Is anything off-limits?"

She swallowed. "Some things are."

"Oh, before I forget. I made you something in wood shop today."

"You did?"

He pulled out a small wooden key chain shaped like a butterfly. The wings were crooked and uneven, but it was sweet and had a very rustic, cool look. A flower from the bank and now a handmade key chain from him?

"Thank you! That's so nice of you."

They slowed down at his math class. "I'll call you later," he said as he let go of her hand.

"We have to start shopping for costumes."

"Yeah." He nodded. "Who knows. Maybe this will be our year." As he walked away, he raised his arms in triumph.

After Natalie got home from school, she had the lovely task of walking Prints William. Grandma Jones explained her lungs couldn't take the stress of a walk, and it was also better if the dog peed on someone else's grass. As compensation, Grandma Jones paid Natalie five bucks a walk. Since Natalie didn't have any income to speak of, thirty-five dollars a week wasn't bad. It didn't fill her gas tank, but it got her to Cold Stone and school.

Many of the neighbors had already begun decorating their yards for Halloween. Plastic skeletons dangled from trees, and about five houses down from Natalie a gigantic blow-up pumpkin covered the neighbors' lawn. For a number of reasons she was sort of looking forward to walking the dog. She liked looking at all the decorations, and she knew it was terrible, but Matt lived a few blocks over. She'd even taken an extra minute to primp before she'd left.

Grandma Jones had asked her why she was putting on lip gloss to walk the dog. Actually, "What the hell are you doing?" had been her exact words. "Putting on makeup to watch Prints William poop on the neighbors' lawn? You must really need some excitement in your life. Why don't you put on makeup for that cute boyfriend of yours? Now, that would be fun."

Natalie had ignored her. However, as she recalled the encounter she wondered if Grandma Jones was right. Maybe what she'd said explained everything about her attraction to Matt. Maybe her life really was just boring. Maybe she had a suppressed need for excitement. Was she only using Matt as a way to spice up her route with Prints William and her mundane school days?

She was heading toward Matt's block at a brisk pace when she noticed a tug on the leash. She turned around to find Prints William lifting his three-inch leg right in front of the Scary Neighbors yard. She always felt uncomfortable whenever he took care of business in anyone's yard, but the Scary Neighbors' yard was the worst. It was the house that never passed out candy on Halloween and had a broken brick wall that looked like actual tombstones all year round—not the fake seasonal ones with cute names that many of her neighbors had decorated their yards with for Halloween. The Scary Neighbors had beat-up cars and dark circles under their eyes.

While she waited for Prints William to pee on their dead grass, she had visions of being attacked with an ax. They didn't seem like the type of people who would understand a little dog sprinkle on their lawn.

"C'mon, Prints," she said quietly. She tugged on the leash, but he still kept peeing, leaving a trail of pee behind him. She felt guilty about dragging him like a rag while he tried to relieve himself. But it was for their own good. If the dog wanted to live, he could suffer for the moment. Relief washed over her when he quit peeing. But her relief faded fast when the dog assumed squat position. She tugged again, hoping she might be able to drag him to the next yard—a landscape filled with lush greenery and a colorful welcome sign that read AUTUMN IS THE SEASON TO GIVE THANKS! But when she pulled on Prints William, he only left a trail of sausagelike poop all over the dead grass, making it worse—and harder to clean up. He looked pathetic being dragged along in squat mode. She figured the best thing to do now was hurry. She shoved her hand inside her pocket for the poop bag she'd brought along with her, only the poop bag wasn't there. She shoved her hand into the other pocket—empty. As she turned out her empty pockets, her heart skipped a beat. She could've sworn she saw the Scary Neighbors' curtain move. Someone was watching her.

The dog, oblivious to her panic, took his time. A rough voice emerged from inside the house. "Get your pooper-scooper! Don't even think about leaving here until you get that poop scooped up! Don't make me come out there!" It was male and sounded like it had spent many days inhaling cigars. She pictured him sharpening his ax while she frantically searched for a pooper-scooper.

Her heart shot into overdrive. She looked around for the voice but there was no one. Did she yell back and sweetly explain that she forgot her pooper-scooper and she'd come back with a weapon and her parents to clean it up? Or did she run for her life?

"Hey, Nat." She'd been so scared she hadn't even heard the engine idling behind her. But she instantly recognized the voice. She spun around and faced Matt, who had an elbow dangling from the side of his truck. He looked happy to see her. If he only knew how happy she was to see him. The only thing she scooped up was Prints William. She ran to the passenger side of his car and jumped in.

"Wait! You little—" She slammed the door before she heard the rest of what Raspy Voice had to say.

She looked at Matt. "Drive."

Matt hit the gas and they were off.

"What was that all about?" Matt asked. "Why were you hanging out in front of the Scary Neighbors' yard?"

She told him all about Prints William deciding to relieve himself in front of the Scary Neighbors. Matt laughed most of the way to her house. "Well, I guess my timing was perfect."

"Thank God you came. They probably would've eaten me for dinner. I can never, ever walk past their house again. They will kill me."

Matt laughed again. "I don't think they'll kill you. But maybe you should make them some cookies to make up for it," he said jokingly. His hair was damp and his eyes looked a little red and bluer than usual. Salt water had this effect on eyes.

"Did you go surfing?" she asked.

He nodded. "I needed a little break."

"You work on the paper a lot."

Prints William put his hind legs on Natalie's lap and propped his front paws on the window. The dog panted as he viewed the scenery outside.

"I think he's looking to see if we're being chased by a man wielding an ax," Natalie said.

Matt laughed again. "What would you have done if I hadn't come?"

"Run for my life."

"You wouldn't have picked it up with your hand? What kind of a neighbor are you?"

"Ewwww!"

"You know I'm kidding."

"Seriously, I think you may have just saved my life." She was just starting to relax a little when she became very aware of the odor in the car, and it wasn't coming from

Matt. She immediately recognized Prints William's fish-butt breath. Worse, it was starting to fog up the windows.

As this horror occurred to her Matt turned the dial on the defroster to high. Then he rolled down his window. What if he thought it was her breath that smelled? Not only did she have mozzarella-crust mouth, but horrendous breath as well? A real princess he'd rescued here. As if he'd ever see her as kissing material. She had to say something.

"Just to let you know, the odor is from Prints William's breath. I'm really sorry. I bet you didn't plan on this when you rescued us."

"Really? I thought that was your breath." He smiled. "I know it's the dog, Nat. It's okay."

"Okay," she said, still embarrassed.

"Let's not forget Ashley."

Ashley was his ninety-pound mastiff. "Her breath is deadly." He laughed. "Seriously, I think it could kill someone. It's toxic."

She tried to feel better.

"Well, it was my pleasure," he said as he pulled into her driveway. "Anytime."

Her heart skipped a beat when she looked at his blue eyes.

He leaned over and reached his arm out. For a moment she thought he was shaking her hand, but his arm went right past her torso. She hadn't been this close to him, and she wondered what he was doing. She held her breath as his fingertip headed for her window. She caught a whiff of the salt water and sunscreen on his skin, and watched as he traced his finger over Prints William's fog on her window. He spelled out WATCH OUT FOR NATALIE'S BREATH.

She slapped his arm. "Thanks a lot." It was something her brothers would do.

He took a minute to laugh at his joke. "I'm just kidding. No, seriously." He put a line through the words with his index finger, then wrote MATT'S RESCUE SERVICE. And beneath it, NATALIE'S SPOT.

The corners of his lips turned up. "Is that better?"

She nodded. It was sweet that he thought that was her spot. But the truth was, that would never be her spot. She felt her heart sink, but forced enthusiasm.

"Much better. Hey, thanks for the lift," she said. "Your timing was perfect." The moment the words left her lips, she realized how ironic they were. In the big picture, his timing couldn't be worse. She was already taken, and any chance they had would be reserved for another lifetime. She watched his car until it was out of the driveway.

After homework and bathing, she headed over to Romeohelpme.

Happy endings
Member: Up All Night
Advanced Member
     I was thinking about what Skater Chick said. Do happy endings only exist in the movies? Really, if you think about it, most happy endings are in movies.

She brushed her teeth, then watched the beginning of *Scream*, knowing the entire time that if she was watching horror movie reruns it was going to be close to impossible to get out of bed in the morning. One, she was staying up too late. Two, these kinds of movies scared her. She'd never be able to fall asleep. But she couldn't resist. The movie was such an escape from her crazy life. People running from a crazed slasher in a freaky mask seemed far worse than having the hots for a guy.

Furthermore, she really wanted to see what her regular bloggers had to say. After she was half-way through the movie, she decided to check.

Member: Glamour Girl
Advanced Member
RE: Happy endings
    I don't think so at all. There are lots of people who find true love.

Member: Dragon Guy
Advanced member
RE: Happy endings
    You're just now realizing that happy endings are only for movies? Where have you been?

Member: Glamour Girl
Advanced Member
RE: Happy endings
    Dragon Guy, what is wrong with you?

Member: New Girl in Town
Newbie
RE: Happy endings
    No kidding, Dragon Guy. There have to be happy endings. Otherwise, there would be no hope in the world.

Member: Skater Chick
Newbie
RE: Happy endings
    But sure, I believe in happy endings.
I guess. Who the hell knows why some
people get lucky and others don't. Some
people get the happy endings. Others don't.

Member: Ralph London
Newbie
RE: Happy endings
    Maybe like the writers of great happy
endings, we create our own destiny with
the choices that we make. Do you have to
"believe" in happy endings? I don't know.
Maybe we just have to believe in ourselves
to find them.

It seemed like no one really knew the
answer. The only thing Natalie knew was
that no one would be able to tell her this for
sure. She was just going to have to find out
for herself.

Eight

Natalie yawned as she stared at the crack in Jeremy's parents' coffee table. She remembered the day the glass had broken. Jeremy had been playing Nintendo Wii on that particular day too. Only that time he'd lost. He'd accidentally dropped the remote thingy on the table, and they'd watched with horror as a crack had spidered down the glass. His dad had moved out several weeks before, but Jeremy had worried his mother was going to flip out. The strange thing was, his mother had never even mentioned it. She wasn't blind, so Natalie had figured that she had been consumed with too many other things to care.

It had been more than two hours since

Natalie had sat down on the couch while Jeremy explained that he just wanted to *quickly* check out his new game. Then they were supposed to begin the quest for Howl at the Moon costumes. With nominations officially out, they needed to get busy.

"Yessss!" he hissed before doing a brief victory dance. She watched his hips rotate in circles as he raised his arms over his head. She giggled as he set the remote down. He dove onto the empty spot next to her. "You ready to go find costumes?" Winning any kind of video game—or really anything, for that matter—always put him in a good mood.

"I've been ready."

"Well, this should make you a little more ready."

She thought he was going to lean in for a kiss. Instead, he jumped into her lap, pressed his bottom against her thighs, and ripped a fart so loud she thought it would shatter the *entire* coffee table.

"Get off me! You are so gross."

Somewhere through his howling laughter she heard her cell phone beep, indicating a text had arrived.

"I'm serious, Jeremy. Get off. You're

sick." He tickled her rib cage and she couldn't help but laugh. In between her squeals of laughter she managed to beg for freedom. "Please! Get! Off!" She gasped for air. "Seriously, I need to get my phone."

Instead of removing his dead weight from her legs, he farted again, laughing even louder. She took a moment to catch her breath before she pushed his shoulders with all her might. He didn't budge. "I can't breathe," she moaned. She could still breathe, but she hoped her desperation would motivate him to take his gas some-place else.

"You're so dramatic!" He laughed.

"I'm serious! Get off! You weigh a thou-sand pounds."

"Have you practiced your speech for the Oscars yet?"

She was saved by his cell phone. He jumped up, immediately fished his phone from his huge pocket, and held it up to his ear. "What's up, bro?"

Natalie wondered who it was. He had a million "bros," Matt being his best bro, of course. "Did you find that part for the truck?"

It had to be Matt. Natalie knew he was

looking for some part for his truck on eBay. While Natalie eavesdropped, she looked at her inbox on her cell phone.

> Just saw Brian at the thrift store looking for Halloween costumes with Kelly. He said they were just going as friends!!! And he liked my shoes!
> XO, Jo

"Oh cool." Jeremy said. "Right on." A pause. "And you said yes." Another pause. "Right on. That should be a good time."

Said yes to what? Natalie wondered. *The dance?* Who had asked him to the dance? She was alarmed by the way her heart rate had shot up. Of course someone had asked him to the dance. He was a total catch. It was bound to happen, and she should be happy for him—not dying of anxiety.

"Well, cool. We're going to look at costumes right now, so I'll let you know if we find any good ones."

There was a pause while Jeremy listened to his friend, and Natalie immediately assumed Matt was sharing his costume ideas. Natalie wondered if he would go as

III

something really cute and couples-driven, or if his date would be just a friend. Was it someone he liked? She still remembered the bashful expression that had come over his face when they discussed his love life on the way to Denny's. It seemed as though he might have a crush on someone, and Natalie couldn't help but wonder if this was that someone. Would they come up with their own ideas and surprise each other right before the dance?

"All right, talk to you later, bro." He clicked his phone shut, then looked at Natalie. "That was Matt." Jeremy shoved his phone in his pocket.

"Oh. How's he?" She tried to sound casual even though she was dying of curiosity.

"Good."

That was it? Good? There had to be more. What had Matt said yes to?

Jeremy grabbed his keys from the table. "I'll drive. You ready?"

Reluctantly, she rose from the couch. She still wanted answers. "So what's Matt up to?" Again, she tried to keep her voice as casual as possible.

Jeremy shrugged. "I don't know. Not

much. He was just leaving school. He found that part for his truck."

Natalie didn't care about the truck. Maybe she had misunderstood the conversation, because Jeremy would've told her if Matt had been asked to the dance. Or at least, she thought he would. Then again, it was Jeremy. He would care more about car parts than dance arrangements.

"Oh, and his parents asked him if he wanted to go to Europe next summer instead of their usual camping trip."

So that's what he'd said yes to. It was only a family vacation. She felt herself relaxing as they headed out the door. Her relief was almost as alarming as her insatiable curiosity. Then she wondered if she had all these crazy feelings because Matt was off-limits. Maybe she was only interested in things she couldn't have. Wasn't that human nature—to always want what you can't have? She remembered the time she'd been shopping with Jo and was debating over a pair of jeans. They were cute, but sort of out of her price range. It wasn't until the salesgirl mentioned that they were the last pair and she'd just taken them off hold for someone else that Natalie made up her mind. She had to have the jeans.

They climbed into Jeremy's Ford Explorer. "What are we looking for today? Any ideas?" he asked.

Natalie kind of liked the idea of Cleopatra. Natalie's hair was similar in style, and after all these years of friends suggesting she go as Cleopatra, she was curious to see what she would look like. "What about Cleopatra and Julius Caesar?"

"Who?" He drove over a large bump as he reversed out of his driveway, and his head jolted as he looked at her.

"You know? Cleopatra and Caesar. One of the most famous couples in history. Or you could go as Mark Antony . . . if you don't like Caesar."

"The singer? And what? You'd go as J.Lo?"

"Not the singer! Those were her boyfriends—Cleopatra's boyfriends. Obviously, you didn't pay attention in history."

"I was thinking that we could go as American Gladiators."

He was dead serious.

She hadn't planned on being cast in a role of female wrestler. She had visions of bright spandex while Jeremy lived out some masculine fantasy that had been brewing in his little mind. Her Cleopatra idea was much better.

"Sorry, but I don't want to be a Gladiator for Halloween," she said.

"Well, I don't want to be some girly-looking Roman guy from history. No thanks."

This wasn't a good start to their Halloween costume–hunting expedition. They weren't even at the costume shop yet. Already, they couldn't agree on anything.

An hour later they stood in front of the dressing rooms in the largest Halloween costume store in San Diego. In spite of Natalie's discomfort she burst out laughing. The spoon costume Natalie wore was so heavy on her body she feared that she would topple over if she so much as breathed, let alone laughed, so she tried to contain herself. Not to mention it was hot. She'd probably sweated off five pounds in the past two minutes alone. So far, the fork and spoon combo seemed to be the only one they could agree on. They'd tried on characters from *Scooby-Doo* and *Star Wars*. Natalie had liked a pair of fifties costumes, but after they had tried them on Jeremy felt like he wasn't "dressed up" enough and had suggested a gangster and flapper combo, which Natalie felt was too overdone.

Jeremy's face peered from beneath the gigantic prongs that stemmed from his head. He checked himself out in the mirror and laughed. "This is hilarious." His legs looked skinny in his black tights, and his head seemed to fit perfectly in the opening for his face.

In spite of their disagreements, they'd still laughed hysterically at some of the crazy things they'd tried on. One thing Natalie had always liked about Jeremy was his willingness to try almost anything. He'd try anything on as long as it didn't involve a skirt. But it wasn't just with Halloween costumes. He was always fun to go to sushi with because he would experiment with more than just California rolls. One time they'd been eating Chinese with some friends and there were all these long, stringy, slimy brown things that looked like worms in their noodles. No one wanted to try them without confirming with the waitress that they weren't worms. But Jeremy stepped up to the plate—literally—and threw a few in his mouth with his bare hands. It had sure made the meal more exciting. "Tastes good," he'd said. It wasn't until the waitress returned that they learned the wormy strings were actually some form of mushroom.

The face opening on Natalie's spoon kept falling over her eyes.

Jeremy chuckled. "That looks a little big on you," he said. "But cute. Maybe they have it in a smaller size."

"I can hardly move."

"I'll go see if they have it in a smaller size."

She watched his chicken legs head for help. Just as he rounded the corner she felt herself teetering. "Wait!" she called. But the face hole had fallen over her mouth and her voice was muffled.

She went down like a statue. Once on the floor, she couldn't move. She tried to roll to the left. But she felt as rigid as concrete. Then to the right. It was the same thing. A song she'd frequently heard at dances went through her head. *To the left . . . To the right . . . Now shake it!* She tried to shake it, but her legs only flailed around like a wounded bee in a swimming pool. She managed to maneuver the face opening up again so at least she could see. "Jeremy?"

No answer, but she could hear his charming voice from somewhere inside the store. She caught bits and pieces. "Vampires are cool . . . a wicked costume . . . western too . . ." She was glad he was discussing costume ideas at length while she lay on the floor like a pillar from the Roman ruins.

It seemed like eons before Jeremy returned. She knew he had come back the moment she heard him laughing. Peals of laughter filled the area behind her. She tried to turn her neck to see him but couldn't.

"Ha. Ha," she said sarcastically. "I'm glad I could entertain you. Now help me up."

"I'm sorry," he managed in between breaths. "But this has to be one of the most hilarious things I have seen in a long time." He came to her side, and when he leaned down she thought he was lending a hand. However, he was doubled over in hysterics.

"Okay, real funny," Natalie said, her tone flat. "Maybe if you take a picture it will last longer."

"That's a great idea," he said, breathless.

She didn't expect him to whip out his cell phone. She was being sarcastic. She was horrified as he held his cell over her in camera mode.

"Jeremy, I swear to God. Help me up. Now I'm annoyed."

"Sorry, sorry," he said as soon as he was finished snapping the picture. He extended his hand, and when she was back on her feet she was horrified to discover that he'd brought company.

The salesgirl was dressed as a witch. Rather than wearing a long cape and gown, she had donned a short little minidress with bell sleeves and a tattered hem. Fishnet tights, a jet-black wig, and, of course, a pointy hat completed the look.

Jeremy looked at the picture on his phone and his body shook with laughter.

"Jeremy! Give me that!" Natalie said. He was so weakened with laughter that he actually handed it over. She thought for sure she would have to attack him to get the picture. She hit delete, guaranteeing the picture would never leave the costume shop. When he finally caught his breath he was able to inform her that the costume was only available in the size she was wearing.

"Sorry," the salesgirl said.

"Natalie, this is Brianna," Jeremy said. "She's in my Spanish class."

Great! She went to their school. She

was hoping that if anyone had witnessed her on the ground—dressed as flatware—it would've been someone she'd never have to see again in her life.

Natalie was afraid to extend her hand or even wave for fear she might end up on the ground as though she'd been tossed on the carpet during a toddler's first meal. Instead, she politely smiled and said, "Nice to meet you."

"Have you guys seen the caveman and cavewoman costumes?" Brianna suggested. "Or there's my favorite—the voodoo doll and the victim."

Only if I can be the doll and not the victim, Natalie thought. "Sure. That sounds cool."

"Let's check it out," Jeremy said, and followed Brianna.

"Jeremy!" Natalie went down again.

"So, did you and Jeremy decide on costumes for the dance?" Natalie's mom asked as she passed a salad bowl around the dinner table.

"Not yet." Natalie took the bowl.

Jeremy had really liked the whole cave-couple idea, but Natalie felt self-conscious in the cavewoman costume. This was mostly because the dress was clearly made for a girl who had been gifted with big boobs, an asset Natalie didn't have. She'd spent her entire five minutes in the outfit continuously pulling up the tube top portion of the minidress, worried she might flash the entire dance floor with her A cups.

"I still have that picture of you two as hippies from last year hanging in my office," her father chimed in.

"Hippies?" Grandma Jones's voice was loud. "Why in the world would you want to go as a hippie? Those people were on drugs, and they smelled. I know what would be a good costume."

Natalie's parents stared at Grandma Jones as they often did when they knew something weird was coming next.

"A roll in the hay! One of you could dress as a dinner roll. And the other could cover themselves in hay. Get it?"

"Mother!" Natalie's mom snapped. "I think that's a little inappropriate for a high school dance. We don't want the kids getting expelled, and what kind of a message does that send?"

Natalie felt her cheeks turning red.

"Oh, Tanya, you need to live a little. As

if kids don't know what a roll in the hay is these days." Grandma Jones shoved a forkful of corn in her mouth.

The truth was, rolling in the hay with Jeremy had been pretty limited to staying outside the barn—period. Natalie always sensed that Jeremy would go further if she let him, but she'd never been quite ready for more than kissing and cuddling. The fact that this had even come up in the presence of her parents was only one more reason to steer clear of Grandma Jones when she'd had more than one gin and tonic before dinner.

"What's a roll in the hay?" one of the twins asked.

Her mother shot Grandma Jones a look. "Now see what you started?"

Due to sheer awkwardness, Natalie wolfed down her dinner and headed upstairs for her nightly routine. Just as she was getting ready to sign on to Romeohelpme, her cell phone lit up. Jo. They'd been playing phone tag back and forth all evening, and they still hadn't had a chance to chat about her Brian encounter at the thrift store.

"Finally!" Natalie greeted her best friend.

"I know. I've been dying to talk to you all day," Jo said.

"So, you ran into Brian at the thrift store?"

"Yes! He looked so cute. And he came up to me first. I didn't even know he was there and suddenly I heard this familiar voice behind me." Jo shared every detail of the encounter, including the color of his shirt. "And he said that Kelly and him were just going as friends."

"In front of Kelly?"

"No. But he said that she has a boyfriend who lives far away and she just asked him as friends."

Natalie couldn't help but think of poor Vincent, who had probably watched Jo grow giddy with delight as she chatted with Brian. "Was Vincent standing there the whole time?"

"No." Her tone changed. "He was kind of weird, actually. I don't know what was up with him. He wandered off, and then after Brian left he came back. But Vincent really didn't even say anything about Brian."

"Gee. I wonder why he was acting weird. It couldn't be because he's had a crush on you since, like, kindergarten."

"No, he doesn't." Jo always denied it, but Natalie knew that deep down she had to realize the truth.

They chatted a while longer about the dance and Brian. Then they somehow got onto the topic of who they would vote for if they were able to vote in the upcoming election, and then discussed the latest celebrity gossip. That was how it was with Natalie and Jo. They could talk about anything and everything and their conversations were always so lengthy and interesting. The girls made plans to hang out after school the next day, and by the time they said good-bye, Natalie was exhausted.

After her shower, Natalie quickly headed to Romeohelpme. Her regular visits were starting to worry her a little. She'd started to become addicted to the posts and replies.

Do we only want what we can't have?
Member: Up All Night
Advanced Member
So I've been wondering, is it human nature to want what we can't have? Are we naturally drawn to things that seem unattainable? I can't help but think of all the times I've wanted something only because there seems to be a shortage. Take pizza day at the cafeteria at my school. It's probably the only day of school when most

of the campus buys lunch. And probably
also the only day when the cafeteria runs
out of food. There never seems to be
enough pizza to go around. Does that make
everyone want it even more? What if we
had pizza every day and there was never
a shortage? Wouldn't we all get sick of it?
Do you think love is the same way? Do we
only want someone when they're intriguing
and unavailable? Then what if you get that
person and you notice all their everyday
habits and you start to get tired of them
like pizza?

Maybe it was the costume hunting, but
she was exceptionally worn out. As she signed
off of the message board her eyes felt heavy.
She set her alarm for a few minutes earlier so
she could check responses in the morning.

Nine

Natalie was still in her pajamas when she logged on to Romeohelpme. She knew that checking her replies would secure her one of the worst parking places on campus, but that didn't stop her.

Member: Dragon Guy
Advanced Member
RE: Do we only want what we can't have?
    Cafeteria food sucks. I would rather go hungry.

Member: Girl Gone Green
Newbie
RE: Do we only want what we can't have?
    I agree with Dragon Guy. Stay out

of cafeterias. The plates are harmful to the environment, and the beef they serve probably comes from mistreated cows. But yes, I agree. We always want what we can't have. My parents would never let me eat candy growing up and something about the intrigue made me want it even more. Then I started stealing it from my grandma's house. My parents found out and they made me write down a hundred reasons why candy is bad for you, and watch some terrible video from our dentist's office. It's when we want what we can't have that we get into trouble.

She had a point. All the things Natalie wanted would only lead to trouble. She read several responses, mostly pointing out that there is something in human nature that makes us all want the unattainable.

Member: Skater Chick
Newbie
RE: Do we only want what we can't have?
Last year I liked a guy I couldn't have for a number of different reasons and one of my best guy friends really liked me but I wasn't interested in my guy friend. He didn't

seem like a challenge, I guess. There was no mystery there. And no chase. It just seemed too easy. But anyway, I finally got the guy that I really liked and he turned out to be different from what I had thought, and then I didn't like him anymore. By the time I realized this I started to have feelings for my friend. But it was too late. He'd already moved on. So be careful. What you want might not always be what you need. And what you need might be right in front of your face.

Natalie wondered if analyzing all these responses would make her crazy. Did all this apply to her life? Perhaps Skater Chick was right. She already had what she needed—Jeremy. She just didn't realize how lucky she was. Maybe all these feelings for Matt were brewing only because of the intrigue. She knew she liked Matt a lot as a friend, but then what if she did have a shot with him and he turned out to be a terrible boyfriend and then she missed Jeremy? Her love life was so confusing. Deep down she knew Matt would be a great boyfriend. It was almost painful to think about how wonderful he would be.

He was going to make someone very happy, and the reality was that it wasn't her.

> **Member: Glamour Girl**
> **Advanced Member**
> **RE: Do we only want what we can't have?**
> Ditto to the end of Skater Girl's message. It sounds just like that tragic movie *Gone with the Wind.* I had to watch it when we were studying the Civil War. Look at how Scarlett O'Hara ended up—alone. You definitely don't want that.

But wouldn't it be better to be alone than with someone she wasn't even sure she liked anymore? Maybe she wasn't even being fair to Jeremy, either. It wasn't very cool of her to hang on to him while she tried to figure out what she wanted. But breaking up with him in the midst of all his family problems would be like adding insult to injury. She didn't know which was worse—not being honest with him, or not being honest with herself.

Natalie looked at the clock. There were several more replies, but she didn't have time to read them, let alone analyze. She had to get moving. She quickly threw her hair in a ponytail, rinsed off, dressed in a pair of jeans and her favorite sweatshirt, then ran to the kitchen for one of her mom's gross cardboard bars she bought at the health food store. Energy bars translated into emergency breakfast or empty pantry; Natalie only resorted to them if she was in a hurry or there was nothing else to eat.

Her brothers were putting on their backpacks in preparation for the school bus. Natalie was just about to dart out the front door when Grandma Jones looked up from *Good Morning America* and called to Natalie.

Natalie spun around. "Yes?"

"You know, Natalie, I was thinking. I have so many old clothes. You kids should take a look at my stuff for Halloween. Don't go spend a lot of money. I bet you could come up with something really good. Or raid your mom's old wardrobe—now, there is something to laugh at."

Natalie knew her mother wasn't Mischa Barton when it came to fashion, but Natalie found her early nineties sense of style more boring than laughable. What would she go as if she raided her mom's wardrobe? A candidate for an *Oprah* makeover segment?

"Okay, thanks," Natalie said. "Maybe I'll have Jo and Vincent come check it out too. They need costumes also." *It probably wasn't a bad idea,* Natalie thought as she headed for the Ravioli.

She obeyed the speed limit even though she risked getting detention. Her parents had always threatened to take the car away if Natalie was ever pulled over for speeding. Losing the car would be worse than detention. She parked in the Outer Space parking lot and had a matter of minutes to sprint to first period. She still had to stop at her locker for her geometry book, but decided not having her book was better than detention, so she went bookless to class and hoped Mr. Lopez would be cool enough to let her have the hall pass. She was rounding the corner when Matt popped his head from his own math class door. It was like he knew she was coming, as if he'd been waiting for her. His hair was still wet from a shower and she could smell soap or shampoo. Guys were so lucky that they didn't have to blow-dry and style hair and could still look clean and prepared after simply showering. She would kill for that luxury. Makeup and her expensive flat iron were must-haves in her life.

"Hey, Nat. I put some more ideas together for our costume article," he said. "I just have to save it to a disk."

She felt out of breath from running. "Thanks."

"I'll get it to you later today, maybe at lunch."

"Sounds good!" She would've loved to stop and discuss his ideas further instead of going to geometry. However, the halls now looked clear of all students and staff—a good sign that the bell was about to ring.

Her foot was barely inside the door when the bell buzzed. "Phew."

Grandma Jones lit a cigarette while Natalie pried open the old trunk. Jo and Vincent sat on the edge of Grandma Jones's bed. Natalie had invited Jeremy to join them, but he was meeting a group of people from his Spanish class to study for a test the next week. Spanish wasn't his favorite subject and she was impressed and surprised that he'd taken the extra time to study for the quiz. It was more Jeremy's style to blow off studying for an afternoon at the skate park. He didn't mind settling for Bs or Cs on tests if it meant he could hang out with his friends. He'd told Natalie to look for "something good" in Grandma Jones's trunk—"but nothing too girly." He'd be interested in whatever she found only if it was cool.

"Don't tell your mom I'm smoking in here." Grandma Jones waved the smoke toward the open window of her bedroom.

"I won't." Her mother probably already knew anyway. Grandma Jones always smoked in her bedroom against Natalie's parents' wishes.

"Where did you get this?" Natalie asked as she pulled out a red, white, and blue top hat.

"Grandpa wore it one year for a Fourth of July parade."

Natalie put it on and her friends began to laugh.

"It's a little crooked," Jo said.

Next Natalie pulled out a gold-sequined one-piece with bell-bottoms and a turtleneck collar. "You wore this?" Natalie asked.

"Oh yes. I wore that in the seventies to a New Year's Eve party. I think there are platform shoes in there to match. I was quite the hit that night."

"That thing is classic," Vincent remarked.

Natalie tossed it to him. "Here. One of you guys can try it on." Vincent passed it to Jo.

"You sure?" Jo held the suit in front of her. "What would Brian think if he saw me in this?"

Vincent was quiet. Jo had never been shy about sharing her feelings around her two best friends. But Vincent always remained quiet whenever Brian came up.

Over the years Natalie and Jo had turned to Vincent as an expert on guys. Back when Natalie had first started hanging out with Jeremy, she'd always asked Vincent questions about guy things, like what kind of Christmas present she should get him or how long she should wait before calling him back. Vincent always had good advice. But whenever Brian came up, Vincent sort of tuned out.

"There's plenty more in here," Natalie said as she began to pull out one thing after another.

Prints William wagged his pinky-shaped tail as he hovered around Jo's feet. Aside from Jeremy, Jo was one of the few people who actually petted Prints William with vigor. Most people patted him gently, then realized their hand reeked so bad they avoided the dog like the plague.

They discovered all kinds of treasures

in the trunk from Grandma Jones's past. She had saved clothes and shoes from every single decade of her life.

"This would make a cool history project," Jo said.

"I was thinking the same thing," Vincent added. "You could make a fashion display at school as a glimpse into several decades with all this stuff."

Sorting through the trunk was a trip down memory lane for Grandma Jones. They pulled out an old Western-style shirt with a matching poufy skirt, and Grandma Jones shared in detail how she used to square dance with a man who later ran for mayor.

They found a beautiful Asian robe. Turquoise blue, it was covered in ornate stitching and came with a matching belt. They also found a karate outfit. Grandma Jones told them how Natalie's grandpa had brought both ensembles back from Japan when he'd been in the army.

Natalie pulled an old bonnet from the trunk. It was dusty and looked like something from the plains, pre–Civil War. "I know you weren't alive when these were in," Natalie said.

Grandma Jones squinted. "What is

that? Oh, that was from when I starred in *Oklahoma!*"

Vincent immediately began singing a tune from the musical and Grandma Jones joined in.

Jo pulled an old wedding dress from the trunk.

"Now, that you can do whatever you want with," Grandma Jones said. "Burn it. Turn it into a tutu. I don't care."

"Isn't this your wedding dress?" Jo asked.

"From my first marriage. You can dye that black for all I care. That husband was useless, and marrying him was like going to a funeral. It's all yours."

It wasn't until they actually started trying on the clothes that the real laughs came out. When Vincent returned from Natalie's bathroom wearing the gold-sequined New Year's Eve pantsuit, the girls couldn't quit laughing. The pants were so tight, and they rode up his behind, giving him a huge wedgie.

"Those look painful," Jo said.

"You kids are crazy!" Grandma Jones said. "I'm going to go watch *Nancy Grace*." Prints William followed her when she left.

The three friends spent a solid two hours trying on Grandma Jones's treasures. They even busted out Natalie's makeup bag and began experimenting with makeup and hair.

Vincent and Jo found success with Grandma Jones's wedding dress. Jo thought it would be fun to go as a bride and groom so long as they could find a cool suit for Vincent. But Vincent suggested they go as a zombie bride and groom. It was a cool idea because the wedding gown looked so old. They were going to paint their faces pale white and put dark circles under their eyes, and Vincent was going to find a really old-looking suit from a thrift store and make it look tattered, as though he'd risen from the dead.

Natalie hadn't found the same success. However, just for fun, she'd tried on the gold disco pantsuit. It was much bigger on her than it had been on Vincent. To top off the outfit she strapped on Grandma Jones's *Oklahoma!* bonnet. The three friends laughed at the combination.

"We have to come up with an *Oklahoma!* disco show tune," Vincent said. It was only seconds before he began singing the

Oklahoma! theme song to the beat of "Stayin' Alive." Natalie and Jo were practically in tears from laughter. He even busted out some disco moves while belting out his song. "I should seriously adapt it for our school. *Oklahoma! The Disco!*" he said. Natalie and Jo laughed even harder.

It was so Vincent to spontaneously come up with something hilarious and creative. Their laughter was disrupted by the doorbell.

"Natalie!" Grandma Jones called. "Can you get that? I ate a salt sandwich for lunch and my ankles are swollen. It's probably that package that I ordered from QVC."

Jo looked at Natalie. "What's a salt sandwich?"

"I have no idea. But I can't answer the door like this." Natalie glanced at herself in Grandma Jones's mirror.

"Sure you can! I dare you to answer the door like that." Jo was still dressed in the old wedding gown.

"No way!"

"Oh, c'mon. You have to. Look at what I'm wearing," Vincent chimed in. He was dressed in a sombrero and a pair of polkadot bell-bottoms.

"Well, then you answer the door," Natalie retorted.

"I didn't dare Vincent," Jo reminded.

"Oh, fine," Natalie said, and groaned.

What's the harm? she thought as she headed to the door. *It's just the UPS man, and he's probably already left the package and is starting up his truck anyway.* Jo and Vincent followed Natalie downstairs, giggling the entire way. The friends hid behind the banister while Natalie opened the door. Instead of finding a package in her driveway she found Matt. The first thing Natalie did was rip off the bonnet. It was a bad move because she could feel her hair standing on end from static.

"Matt! What are you doing?" she asked as she tried to push flailing strands of hair down with her hands.

He looked her up and down. "More like, what are *you* doing?"

"Jo and Vincent are over, and we were looking for Halloween costumes."

Jo and Vincent waved to Matt from behind the banister. Their outfits were safely hidden, but the expressions they wore suggested that they were loving every minute of this.

Matt tilted his head to one side with

curiosity. "Don't take this the wrong way, but what were you thinking of going as?"

She felt so silly. "Uh, I'm not sure. We were just messing around. I was just trying on a bunch of stuff."

"Pretty original costume," he said, showing his dimples. "You're like *Little House on the Prairie* meets disco." He nodded. "It could work."

She chuckled nervously. "Trust me, I'm not going as this. We were just messing around."

"Hey," Matt said, lowering his voice as he glanced at Jo and Vincent. "Can you talk for a sec? Maybe outside?"

She glanced over her shoulder at her friends. She could tell they were straining to hear. Then she turned back to Matt. "Yeah, sure." Her first thought was Jeremy. Maybe he needed to confide that Jeremy was consumed with depression over his parents and they had to do something extra special for his birthday this year. Then she realized it was probably just the column he wanted to discuss.

The bell-bottoms were a little long and dragged on the welcome mat. She closed the door behind her.

"So while I was thinking about the

couples costume piece I was thinking that maybe we should turn it into another column. Have multiple columns this month. Since the column has become so popular, Mr. Moore thought it was a great idea. And someone else wrote in with another question. We thought you could answer three questions this month. If the response is good, we might have you start answering several questions a month with short, simple advice."

"Um, okay. Sure." They were giving her more column duties? Just what she needed.

"Great. I thought you'd be okay with it. We've already done half the work on the couples costume idea, so you just have to adapt as though you're giving advice."

"Okay, I hear ya."

He pulled a disk from his backpack, then handed her an envelope. "Here's the other question that someone wrote in with." All the questions that came in for the column went into a small, locked suggestion box for the newspaper. Comments and ideas for other articles were also thrown into the box. "Please don't let Jo and Vincent see the question. They'll figure out what it was for, and then the whole cover for the column would be ruined."

She pictured Jo and Vincent with their ears pressed to the front door, trying to eavesdrop. They had to be wondering what in the world she was doing outside with Matt. She couldn't blame them if they had turned Nancy Drew. It was a little odd that she was standing in her front yard sweating her buns off in a relic from the disco era while discussing a covert love column with Matt.

"I promise I won't let them see." She tucked the envelope into a small pocket on the side of the pantsuit, then patted her hip for good measure. "It's safe inside there."

She said good-bye to Matt and returned to her friends.

Jo raised her eyebrows the second Natalie entered. "'Talk for a sec'? 'Outside'?"

"What was that all about?" Vincent asked, equally interested. "Are you guys planning a coup d'état at the newspaper? Is there some scandalous article you're going to break next week? 'Rat Tail Found in Cafeteria Food'?"

Natalie laughed and shook her head. "No. It had nothing to do with the paper. It was just something about Jeremy. Matt's worried because of all his family issues. I guess he just felt funny talking about it in front of you guys." She hated lying to her best friends but if she told them it had to do with the paper they'd put two and two together. Everyone on campus had always wondered who was behind the column and everyone knew that she wrote the occasional feature article for the paper. Jo and Vincent were no dummies.

This answer seemed to satisfy them. "Poor Jeremy," Jo said.

Vincent commiserated. "I know how the guy feels."

They headed back upstairs, and Natalie went into the bathroom to peel off the disco suit and change into her regular clothes.

Once dressed, she sat down on the edge of the bathtub and pulled the envelope from her pocket. The envelope was sealed. What's more, the anonymous writer had gone so far as to seal the envelope with a Spider-Man stamp. It was a weird choice, but clearly this person wanted their problem kept secret. She was torn between dread and curiosity. Dread over coming up with advice and curiosity over what the writer had felt was so secret that they needed to seal the envelope with a stamp. The letter was typed, as most were. Advice seekers were very on the down low with their queries. They were so cautious about revealing their identities that even handwriting was almost always kept secret.

> Dear Coyote Courtship,
>   I have feelings for someone, but if I were ever to act on them I would disappoint and hurt several other people that I care about. This person is taken. In other words, belongs to someone very close to me. What should I do? I don't want to hurt anyone but I can't help the way I feel either. Furthermore, I can't stop thinking about this person. Everything just feels so natural when I'm with this individual, but I feel like a bad person for even having these thoughts. Any insight you have would be greatly appreciated.
>   Yours truly,
>   Stuck Between a Rock and a Hard Place

There were a million different ways to answer this, and none of the options she had in mind struck her as the right answer. However, the hardest thing about reading the note was that it felt as though she had written the letter herself. She'd already gone over every possible option in her mind. She wasn't even sure if a good answer existed.

Ten

Dear Stuck Between a Rock and a
Hard Place,

You have a number of options, so I will
sum them up in one response.

Option A: Hurt the people you care
about, come across as a major lame-o
to the rest of the world while following
your heart.

Option B: Hurt yourself and remain
quiet.

Option C: Give it time and see what
happens. Maybe everything will work
itself out.

Natalie highlighted the text and hit
delete. She couldn't use this for the column.

It was hardly an answer. She had to write what Rock and a Hard Place wanted to hear. Just like Natalie, this person was looking for an answer, not a bunch of options that he or she had probably already pondered at length. But the truth was that Natalie didn't know the answer. Any answer she came up with would be a win-lose situation. There was no win-win situation when you had feelings for someone who was off-limits. She decided to set the column aside for a while and focus on something more fun and productive—something she did have answers for. The quiz for the newspaper.

After Jo and Vincent had left with their Halloween costumes last night, she'd written a first draft for the quiz, and had a blast doing it. The only thing was, she wasn't sure if the quiz worked. It was the first personality quiz she'd ever created, and she was afraid that the scores would come out all convoluted. So she'd sent the first draft to her two best friends and her boyfriend. She had predictions about how all three would score.

If the quiz was a success, she would show it to Matt. She wasn't sure how he would score. He was such a well-rounded person. She'd found ambiguous results for herself as well. When she had taken the quiz, her results almost could've fallen into any of the five categories. However, she'd had a slight edge in one category. She didn't know whether she should take this as a sign that she was messed up or that the quiz was.

Just to refresh her memory, she read the quiz one more time before reading their e-mails.

What Is Your Halloween Style?

1. As a kid you went trick-or-treating as one of the following:
    A. a vampire or a witch
    B. a princess or a pirate
    C. a pumpkin or a cute animal
    D. a baseball player, in your softball or little league uniform
    E. Your parents forced you to wear their lame costume ideas.

2. On your list of costume ideas for this year's dance you're considering:
    A. something that will result in terrified glances from classmates
    B. matching costumes for you and your date

C. originality

D. an important historical figure

E. watching a horror movie marathon—
school dances are stupid

3. Which of the following costume ideas appeals
to you the most?

A. Jigsaw from the Saw movies

B. Cinderella or Jack Sparrow

C. Napoleon Dynamite

D. Danica Patrick or Tiger Woods

E. If you were to dress as something—
which you never would—it would have
to be totally original.

4. Which of the following best describes your
perfect Howl at the Moon experience?

A. preparty with Red Bull and the latest
System of a Down CD before heading
to the dance for pictures only (your date
insists)

B. your dream date (the one you were
hoping to go with since summer), a limo,
tons of pictures, dinner at a beachside
restaurant

C. a fantastic date with other fun couples—
the more the merrier, right?—fun
costumes, and a meal at Friday's

D. The dance will be fun, but you're more
   focused on SAT scores.
E. There is so much more to life than
   this dance.

5. You hope your Howl at the Moon pictures:
   A. give people nightmares
   B. are perfect to carry around in your wallet,
      send to your out-of-state cousins, and
      add to your collection of framed photos
   C. capture all your memories with your best
      friends so you can laugh every time you
      look at them
   D. fit nicely into your memory box
   E. You just hope you don't have to look
      at everyone else's Howl at the Moon
      pictures.

If you scored:
Mostly As, you are **Dressed to Kill**
Mostly Bs, you are **Dressed to Dream**
Mostly Cs, you are **Dressed to Impress**
Mostly Ds, you are **Dressed for Success**
Mostly Es, you are an **Anarchist**

Dressed to Kill. If you answered mostly As,
you love Halloween because it's the only time
of year you can get away with scaring everyone

to death. A free-spirited daredevil, you find enjoyment in doing things that most people shy away from. You don't worry often, and you'd be the first person to run into a burning building to rescue your friends.

Dressed to Dream. You've been planning for the Howl at the Moon dance long before bids went on sale. You've had a date in mind, and coordinating costumes have been brewing in your head since summer. You spend most of Spanish and math daydreaming about the future. Luxury cars, a soul mate, and nothing but bliss are all part of your fantasies.

Dressed to Impress. You're the fun-loving friend who everyone wants in their Howl at the Moon limo. Your Halloween costumes vary between original and hilarious and always have your own personal flair. You love dances because you can hang out with your friends and tear up the dance floor. Your creative and positive attitude gives you an eclectic mix of friends. You're the life of the party.

Dressed for Success. You've probably made honor roll since kindergarten. You like to dress up as things that you wish you could be. High-profile sports figures, celebrities, or superheroes top your list of ideas. You study a lot and you're also a little anxious to graduate.

The Anarchist. So you have a style that's all your own and it doesn't involve school dances and holidays that excite mainstream society. But just because you pass up the kind of stuff that's for sheep doesn't mean you aren't wickedly creative. You're understated now, but you'll be the rock star or the next Kat Von D everyone says they once knew.

Not bad, Natalie thought. She was proud of her work, and she only hoped her friends had fit snugly into one category. She opened Vincent's e-mail first.

To: Natalie Dean
From: Vincent Menino
RE: The quiz
    What's up, Natty? I guess I'm "dressed to dream." Looking forward to that luxury car and my dream girl. Cool quiz. Call u later.

This was exactly what she would've predicted for Vincent. She was excited that the quiz had worked. She was afraid everyone else would score all over the map, as she had.

To: Natalie Dean
From: Jo Agassi
RE: The quiz

   OMG! I love this quiz! This is so
me!! How did you know I was dressed
to dream? It was like you wrote the quiz
just for me. You know I've secretly always
wanted to go as Jasmine from *Aladdin*.

Natalie smiled to herself. Another predic-
tion turned out correctly. She should be the
one reading teacups. She knew Jo would end
up in the dreamer category. In fact, she'd had
Jo in mind when she'd written the profile.
She was just relieved that the quiz was a success. And the fact that Jo and Vincent were
both "dressed to dream" was just one more
reason that they were perfect for each other.
They were like the male and female version
of each other. Now she just wished Jo could
see that Vincent was right for her.

   She opened Jeremy's e-mail last.

To: Natalie Dean
From: Jeremy Maddox
RE: The quiz

   What up, Nat? Please don't make
me take any more of these girly quizzes.

I guess I'm dressed for success. I'm
out. L8R.

Dressed for success? What? She had
banked on dressed to impress or even dressed
to kill. But dressed for success? This just
went to show how much she didn't know
him. Since when did he care about SAT
scores? He was practically failing Spanish.
Was there a hidden overachiever inside of
him that she hadn't met yet? Not only were
Natalie's results different from his, but he'd
completely surprised her. She sighed as she
closed out her computer screen. She was
more confused than ever.

Tomorrow she would finish the costumes
column and try to return to Stuck Between a
Rock and a Hard Place. She saved the quiz to
a disk and put it in her backpack. She would
deliver it to Matt at lunch the following day.
She was dying to know what he thought.

It was a daily ritual for Natalie to head from
French toward Jeremy's Spanish class after the
bell signaled lunchtime. This route would
take her to Jeremy and then on to the cafeteria for lunch, where they would meet with
all their friends. Jeremy hated to wait for

anything, so he usually headed in her direction even though it was backtracking for him. Today she didn't see his silhouette headed in her direction. She was so used to seeing his backpack slung over his shoulder and his skateboard tucked under one arm that it felt a little strange and lonely without his presence. Had he forgotten about her? Was he staying behind for extra help? One time when he'd been out of school sick for three days he'd stayed behind to catch up on his assignments, but he hadn't been sick lately.

Crowds of students headed in various directions, but most were also headed toward the cafeteria. Through the herds she spotted her boyfriend. He stood outside his classroom door talking to someone. She weaved her way in and out of traffic, and he didn't seem to notice her until she was standing right next to him. He had his iPod out, and one earphone was attached to his ear and the other to the ear of the girl who stood in front of him.

"Oh, hey," he said. "You remember Brianna."

Natalie looked at the girl's dimples and thought she seemed eerily familiar. Then it hit her. She was the girl who'd helped them at the costume shop. She looked different when she wasn't wearing a jet-black wig and a witch's hat. "Oh yeah." She smiled. "How's it going?"

"Great!" Brianna beamed. "Good to see you again."

"I hardly recognized you," Natalie said. "I would've never known you were a blonde."

She nodded. "I know. They make us dress up at work. We rotate costumes. Today I have to go as a rabbit!" She laughed, then pulled the earphone from her ear. She turned to Jeremy. "Thanks for letting me hear that. I love it."

"I was just letting Brianna check out the new Slipknot song. I uploaded it last night."

"Cool," Natalie said. She was glad someone could appreciate his music. Natalie thought that most of what he listened to sounded worse than a car accident. She would rather listen to screeching tires than the sound of the Slipknot lead singer's voice, if you could even call him a singer. He was more like a screamer. All the guy did was yell in the microphone. She couldn't even understand what he was saying. She'd tried for a long time to think Jeremy's music was as cool as he did. But the truth was the sound of the hammering drums and screech-ing guitar only made her nervous.

"Brianna just moved here from Florida over the summer," Jeremy said.

"How do you like it here so far?" Natalie asked as they headed toward the cafeteria.

She nodded. "I like it. I miss home a little—and all my friends."

"Why don't you eat lunch with us today?" Natalie suggested.

"Really?" She seemed surprised.

"Sure," Jeremy chimed in. He slid his hand into Natalie's.

"You guys are the first people who have asked me to eat lunch with them. I usually just go to the library and study so I don't have to look like a total loner." Hearing that made Natalie sad. She put herself in Brianna's shoes. She couldn't imagine leaving Jo and Vincent. Even the thought of leaving Jeremy made her feel a little heartsick. Just because she had doubts about him as a boyfriend didn't mean that she didn't care about him. She wanted him in her life no matter what.

"It must be hard to move so far away from all your friends. I would've been scared," Natalie said.

As soon as they found their lunchtime

hangout, Natalie introduced Brianna to the group. Between Jeremy and Natalie they had a big group of friends, and their posse usually took up the whole left corner of the quad. Of course there were Matt, Jo, and Vincent. Jo had all her friends from the dance committees that she worked on. Vincent had various friends from his drama and art classes. Vincent was the type of person who made friends everywhere he went, and he was always hitting it off with shy classmates who found it hard to fit in. Everyone loved Vincent. Then there were all of Jeremy's friends from baseball and the ones he skateboarded with. Brianna seemed to fit in well. Natalie caught glimpses of her chatting with some of the guys, and she overheard Jo telling her about the best places to buy shoes in the area.

Natalie had packed her lunch in haste, and it consisted of a Diet Coke, a string cheese, and a peanut butter and jelly sandwich. She only bought lunch on pizza day. The cafeteria food was just too greasy and questionable for her. She always ate her lunch next to Jeremy. They'd perch up on the quad wall and after they finished eating, they'd hop off the wall and mingle with friends.

As soon as Natalie had thrown out her

trash, she delivered the disk to Matt. She figured that the best time to hand it over was when a ton of other people were around. That way he couldn't ask her how the column was going. She didn't really want to tell him that she couldn't come up with an answer to the question he'd given her that day in the driveway. The author of the quiz would be no secret, as the column was. Her byline would go beneath the quiz, so it was safe to discuss around their friends.

He was munching on a bag of chips and set them down to take the disk.

"It's just the quiz. I'll try to give you the rest tomorrow."

He perked up. "Great. I can't wait to read *the rest*. I'm sure it's great." He tucked the disk into his backpack. "So, I was walking my dog last night and the Scary Neighbors asked me if I'd seen you."

"Get outta here," Natalie said, and smiled.

"No, seriously." His expression was flat and for a moment Natalie thought he might be telling the truth. "They said they wanted you to come back and clean up your dog poop. They know where you live."

"Matt, this is so not funny. You better be kidding."

He chuckled. "No. I didn't see the Scary Neighbors. But I made a point to walk on the opposite side of the street just in case my dog had to lay one on their lawn."

The bell rang and Natalie said good-bye to Matt. She was grabbing her backpack when Brianna approached. "Thanks for inviting me today," she said.

"Sure. Where are you headed?"

"The E building. I have English now."

"Cool. I have art in the F building. Let's walk over there together."

Jeremy gave Natalie a quick peck on the lips before he headed to PE. "I'll call you after school," he said. "Maybe we can grab a Cold Stone."

"Sounds good," she said.

The campus was always a bit messy after lunch. Trash cans were filled and the occasional breeze sent empty lunch bags and food wrappers flying. Natalie avoided stepping in a puddle of soda near the end of the quad. Fliers for the dance covered nearly every square inch of free wall space.

They chatted about some of Natalie's friends. Brianna had questions about who was dating whom. She seemed to really like everyone.

"This was the best day I've had at this school so far," Brianna said

"I'm glad," Natalie said.

"You should come to the costume shop again." Brianna ran her fingers through her hair. "I can give you my employee discount. I'm only supposed to use it for two costumes, but seeing as how I probably won't have a date to the dance, you and Jeremy can use it."

"That's really sweet of you." Natalie barely avoided stepping in gum. "But we'll find you a date. Jeremy has a million cute friends to choose from."

Brianna shrugged. "They are cute. But I'm so new. No one knows me."

They reached Brianna's building first and said good-bye before parting ways.

Just as Natalie was nearing her class Matt came running up from behind. "Hey, Nat," he said. "Do you want to meet at Denny's tomorrow to discuss the rest of the stuff for the paper?"

She smiled. "Sure. I'd love to."

"I have to pick up my brother at football practice. So let's say four?"

"Sounds good."

As he walked away she tried to tell herself that she wasn't excited.

Eleven

Matt was waiting for her at Denny's when she arrived. He'd already ordered a basket of cheese fries and two drinks.

She slid into the booth across from him. "Thanks for all this," she said.

"I figured you'd be hungry. And you deserve it after picking up all that extra work. I think this issue of the paper will be one of the best since I started working on it last year."

"That's good to hear." She hoped he wasn't too disappointed to learn that she hadn't completed all her responsibilities.

"Love the quiz," he said. "It's great. Everyone is going to love it."

She felt proud and was relieved that he

liked it. Writing anything always made her feel a little vulnerable and self-conscious, and his opinion was especially important to her. "How'd you score?" she asked.

"I could've gone a few different ways, but in the end I had the most for dressed to impress. It was only questions two and three that put me in that category."

His response caused her to gasp and she began choking on a cheese fry. She didn't know what she wanted more—to live or die—as she reached for her throat and tried to dislodge the fry.

"Oh my God, Nat. Are you okay?" He jumped from the booth, and knocked over her Diet Coke in the process.

He slapped her back and she felt her eyes watering.

She hadn't expected his quiz results to instigate the Heimlich maneuver. She so didn't want to be choking. Not just because she didn't want to die on a Denny's floor in Oak Canyon, but also because it was the most unflattering look in the world. She could just feel her face growing beet red and her eyes uncontrollably welling up with water. And what if the cheese fry popped from her throat and landed on Matt?

"Help!" he called.

From out of nowhere, the largest woman Natalie had ever seen in her life appeared. She wore a Denny's uniform, and each boob alone looked bigger than Natalie's head. "Meaty" came to mind. This full-figured superhero grabbed her like a Barbie, put her in a backward bear hug, and squeezed the living daylights out of her. A gnarled-looking cheese fry landed on the table, and Natalie was just thankful it hadn't landed on Matt's shirt.

By now the entire east section of Denny's was watching her.

"You all right?" Matt asked as he placed his hand on her shoulder.

"Fine," she croaked. But Helga the Heimlich Hero kept on squeezing. Natalie's feet dangled above the ground like two little puppet legs.

"Get it out. Get it out," the waitress said.

"It's out." Natalie gasped. "You can put me down now."

Helga gave her one more squeeze and Natalie felt her hair flopping in all kinds of directions.

"Thanks," she managed to say as Helga set her down. "I think you saved my life."

"You won't be the first," Helga said, before offering to bring her another drink.

Natalie's voice was hoarse when she spoke. "I'm so embarrassed," was all she could muster.

"It's okay," Matt said. "You sound like a rock star with that voice. Like you've been partying all night. It's kinda cool."

She couldn't help but smile. It was very nice of him to see the good in this horrifyingly shameful experience. And to be a rock star in his eyes, no less. She'd felt like a freak of nature. She slid back into the booth and waited for her new Diet Coke.

"I don't know what happened. I guess I just breathed the wrong way." *I guess you just shocked me nearly to death when you told me we scored exactly the same on the quiz*, she thought. *Exactly the same.*

"I've done that before. It was in a Chinese restaurant—beef with broccoli. The beef almost did me in."

"Really?

"Yeah, you know how beef can sometimes get stuck together with one thin string of meat?"

She nodded even though she didn't want to talk about choking anymore.

She hoped the sooner she got them off the topic of choking, the sooner he'd forget about Helga waving her around like a rag doll. She cleared her throat. "Let's talk about the quiz."

"Oh yeah. I showed it to Mr. Moore, who, by the way, loved it. He thought it was a really fun idea. And he scored dressed to dream."

"Mr. Moore? Who woulda thought?"

Matt nodded. "I know. I mean, I never would've imagined that balding little Mr. Moore with his pencils in his front pocket has Jack Sparrow inside him—just waiting to swashbuckle."

She laughed, and the laughing made her dry throat coarse. She began to cough. "What is swashbuckling, anyway?" she asked in between coughs.

He shrugged. "No clue. Just thought it sounded appropriate."

"You know he recites lines from the movie in front of the mirror every night."

Matt burst out laughing. "That's a pretty funny thought."

They joked about their journalism teacher a little more before Natalie retrieved a disk from her backpack.

"Here's the costumes column." A busboy set her Diet Coke on the table and Natalie thanked him. "And . . . I didn't quite complete the . . . *other* . . . column . . . yet." She explained, "I just, I don't know. I couldn't seem to come up with an answer to fit the question. I didn't think it was fair to make something up." Natalie shook her head. "Maybe you can come up with something better."

She slid the disk across the table. He looked at the envelope, then back at her. He was quiet and she wondered if he was disappointed. She continued explaining. "But I just . . . this one was hard. It's not that I don't think I could *ever* come with an answer, but the right one just hasn't hit me. If you want to tell Mr. Moore and he wants to give me a bad grade, fine. But I feel too weird giving this person advice when I don't even know if it's good advice."

He nodded. "I understand. And I appreciate your honesty. It's okay, Nat. I won't tell Mr. Moore. I'll tell him you've done a great job. And that's the truth." She sensed that he was a little disappointed that she hadn't completed all her work. He was diligent and passionate about the newspaper and his writing. She hated to let him down, but in her heart she knew she was doing the right thing. "I guess it would be hard to find an answer for that one," he mumbled.

"Then you understand?"

He nodded. "Of course."

They talked about the paper a bit more. Then conversation drifted to topics that were non-school-related. Talking to Matt was almost like talking to Jo or Vincent. She had the right vibes with him. They saw eye to eye on almost everything. She would get so excited when he would share a similar like or dislike because some of the things he said were words taken from her own mouth. He liked to write too, which was a bonus because she didn't know anyone else who shared the same passion.

"I just wrote a short story," Matt said.

"That's so cool. What's it about?" She took a sip of her soda.

"It's kind of scary. And it's true."

"Now I'm intrigued."

"I wrote about how I was camping with my brother and my dad over the summer. We were fishing way out in the middle of nowhere and we decided to head back to our campsite kind of late. It was getting dark and there wasn't a single solitary soul around. And we were walking along and there was this guy just sitting there on a rock. It was almost like he'd been watching us before we even saw him. It kind of gave me the creeps. You should've seen where we were. I'm talking pine trees taller than skyscrapers in every direction for miles and a windy trail at least five miles from the highway."

The waitress came to check on them and Matt paused. Natalie felt a little freaked out already. "What happened?" she asked as soon as the waitress was gone.

"We started talking to him and he was nice. He said he was looking for his horse. He didn't have a fishing pole or even a backpack. Instead, he carried this old-looking saddle. His clothes were Western style and they seemed old too. I've never seen anything like his cowboy hat or boots before. And then in the middle of our conversation we heard rustling in the bushes behind us, and when we turned to look, there were two deer." He paused to pop a cheese fry in his mouth.

"That's cool. It's not often you see deer right next to you." Natalie remembered the time she went to Jackson Hole with her family and they saw a moose standing right on the side of the road. It was so close she could've reached out and touched it. "So, what happened with the man?"

"Well, this is the freaky part," Matt continued. "When we turned around, the man was gone. Nothing—no sign of him. We were really quiet and we didn't even hear footsteps. He just vanished. And this is the scariest part of all. When we got back to camp, we told one of the guys who worked at the campground about it and he said horses aren't allowed on those trails. He hadn't seen a horse in more than twenty-five years."

Chills ran up her spine. "You think you saw a ghost?"

He shrugged. "I don't know. Maybe. I'd feel like a total nut telling most people that, but I swear even my dad, the most level-headed person in the world, thought it was eerie."

"That's freaky, Matt. Really, that is scary." She took the last sip of her drink and the last drops of liquid running up the straw sounded like a garbage disposal.

"I haven't told many people about it, but

I think I want to put the story in this issue of the paper."

"It's perfect for this issue of the paper! And what better story for Halloween? Even if I tried to imagine a story better than that I couldn't. Why didn't you tell Jeremy and me this story before?"

"I don't know. Jeremy would probably laugh. And I didn't want people to think I was crazy. It's so weird, you know?"

She shook her head. "I don't think you're crazy. I totally believe you."

He reached inside his backpack. "Will you read it for me? You have such a good eye for detail and I need an honest opinion."

She was flattered. "Of course. I'd love to. As long as it doesn't scare me to death. Is this going to keep me up all night?"

He shrugged and grinned mischievously. "It might."

After the fries were finished, they headed out to the parking lot together and Natalie began to think about how each time she was with him she wished it would last a little longer. Then that horrible conflicted, guilty feeling sunk in, and she told herself that maybe she shouldn't have any more meetings with Matt. Really, it was probably best if she just stayed away from him.

"Nat?"

She swung her head around to face him.

"I just said your name twice and you didn't even hear me."

"Really? I just spaced out, I guess."

"You realize that you did that last time we were here too?" The wind rustled tree branches behind him.

She remembered the incident in his car.

"I don't know what's wrong with me. Maybe I'm going deaf. Sorry."

Maybe I'm going deaf? Where did she come up with these things? Sometimes she thought her mouth acted before her brain.

"What's up with you these days, Nat? You don't seem like yourself."

"Really? I mean, nothing really. I just have a lot of homework. And with Jeremy's birthday planning and the Halloween dance coming up I've been overwhelmed."

"You sure you're just overwhelmed? You seem, I don't know, kinda sad or something."

"Just overwhelmed." She nodded. "I'm sure."

A silence followed, and she sensed that

he knew she was lying. Their eyes locked and something about the way he looked at her made her feel like she could spill. She just started talking. She couldn't help it.

"Well, I guess things have been a little weird. I just feel so conflicted all the time, like I'm trying to make everyone else happy and I'm not doing what I really want to do. Do you ever feel that way?"

"Maybe a little with my parents. I mean, when my mom used to make me put on dorky Christmas sweaters for church on Christmas."

He didn't get it. There had been a moment when she thought he'd understand, but her problems went deeper than Christmas sweaters.

Then he changed his tune. "But no, I see what you're saying," he said. "When I was a freshman, my parents wanted me to take all these math classes. I think they were really hoping to prepare me for a different path. They went to MIT. It was sort of hard for them to understand that I hate that kind of stuff. I love writing and books. They even asked me what I was going to do with writing, as if writing was a really stupid career path."

Maybe he did understand how she felt. She knew his parents had boring jobs—she wasn't even sure what they were. She knew that he was passionate about writing, but she'd never known that he felt so conflicted behind closed doors. From the outside, Matt always seemed so happy-go-lucky. A breeze stirred the dusky air and Natalie hugged her bare shoulders. She'd worn a tank top to their meeting, but now that the sun was starting to disappear it felt freezing in the parking lot.

"Do you want to sit inside the car for a sec?" He pointed to the Ravioli.

"Sure." She unlocked the doors and he climbed into the passenger seat. It was quiet and warm inside the car—the noise of traffic from the cross street was gone, and there were no more rustling branches. "So how did you get out of dealing with all the pressure from your parents . . . without totally hurting them?"

"It was hard. I just realized they were going to be a little hurt. But that's life. You can't spend your entire life pleasing everyone. You'd never do what you were meant to do."

"I guess. But my situation is so different.

I think I will really hurt feelings." They were quiet for a moment. She felt like she could confide in him—friend to friend. "If I tell you something, you promise you won't say anything or judge me?"

"I would never repeat anything you told me. And I would never think badly of you. Ever."

Was he always this sincere? In that moment she felt she could confide.

She started slowly. "Well, it's Jeremy." Deep breath. "You know I care about him so much. But for a long time now I think we've just . . . I guess I've just been more aware of our differences. It seems like we're so different and I keep thinking he would be perfect if I could just change a few things. But I can't change him, and the last thing I want to do is change him." Matt listened, and she continued. What came next was the hardest part to admit to Jeremy's best friend. "I think I need a break. But with all that he's been going through, the last thing I want to do is hurt him."

Matt sighed and gazed out the windshield. For a moment she felt like she shouldn't have said anything. It had been a mistake confiding in him. What was she thinking? Imagine if Jo had a boyfriend and he basically told Natalie that he needed a break from her best friend. Natalie would feel horrible. It would put her in such an awkward spot. Talk about pressure. Look at the kind of pressure she'd just placed on Matt. It wasn't like he was going to tell her to follow her heart with this one. On the other hand, she wasn't sure how Jeremy really felt either. After all, maybe Matt knew something she didn't know. Before Jeremy's parents dropped their bombshell, she thought he might have been thinking of taking a break too.

"I guess it's just so hard for me to imagine anyone else with Jeremy, and vice versa. I think he's great for you."

She had been such an idiot. Now she just looked ungrateful. Everyone thought Jeremy was great for her and she seemed to be the only person who doubted it. She probably sounded whiny to Matt. Good ol' Matt, who always appreciated what he had and went with the flow, was probably only lending an ear to a friend who needed someone to talk to, and she'd taken it too far.

"Yeah, you're right," she said. "I guess I just need to be reminded sometimes."

There was no good answer for what he'd said. She felt foolish. *Reminded sometimes?* Who had to be reminded that she liked her boyfriend? "Well," she said, "thanks for listening." She turned the key in the ignition. "I should probably head home. I told my parents I would be home by now."

He nodded. "Me too." He climbed from the car.

She wished she could rewind and place herself back in Denny's. She would've never told him the truth.

Twelve

"Did you hear me?" Jeremy sounded irritated. "Hello? Am I talking to myself? I always love having conversations with myself."

Natalie set down her sandwich and turned to her boyfriend. "Oh, sorry. I was just spacing out." *Again?* she thought. First with Matt and now with Jeremy. Just yesterday she'd done this to Vincent. After she had come back to earth, Vincent had said he'd told her that the girls' bathroom in the F building was on fire and Justin Timberlake was putting it out, and she hadn't even flinched. Of course the bathroom hadn't been on fire and Justin Timberlake was probably romancing Jessica Biel somewhere in Hollywood, but that's how out of it she'd been. She hadn't heard one word of Vincent's story about his drama teacher. Now she was not only a terrible girlfriend, but a terrible friend, too.

"That's a real interesting scene you were staring at there," Jeremy said sarcastically.

"I wasn't even really watching anything," she said. "I was just zoning." Her eyes had been fixed on Brianna and Travis, but her thoughts had been on Matt. It had been three days since their Denny's encounter and they hadn't spoken a word to each other ever since. She didn't want to be paranoid, but it seemed like he was avoiding her. He hid in the newsroom for most of the lunch period, and whenever he did show up to lunch it was only to grab food from the cafeteria. If he did stick around for a few minutes he was surrounded by friends.

"What were you thinking about?" Jeremy asked.

"All these quizzes I have coming up." She hated lying and quickly changed the subject. "What's up?"

"I was just wondering if you invited Brianna to my party."

The party. The truth was, she'd hardly done anything for the party. Guilt consumed her. She swallowed. "I was going to," she said. "I will."

She set down her drink and noticed that Matt had shown up for a change. He was talking to Brianna and Travis, and she wondered what they were all laughing about. She didn't mean to stare, and when he turned his gaze in her direction she quickly looked away.

She'd read his ghost story the same night he'd given it to her. Despite the fact that the story had kept her up until four in the morning, she'd loved it. She hated to admit it, but she had to watch the Cartoon Network just to desensitize herself from fear. She couldn't even log on to Romeohelpme. Every noise she'd heard in her house made her nerves jump. She'd been dying to discuss the story with Matt, but his random appearances had made it impossible. Every time she had tried to approach him, he was talking to someone else.

She saw him head to the cafeteria line and hoped that today she might find an opportunity to chat with him. Maybe discussing the story would get rid of the awkwardness that seemed to exist between them. They could discuss writing as usual and pretend as if the

Denny's parking lot conversation had never taken place.

She waited until he returned from the food line with a burrito that looked as though it had suffered a trauma in the cafeteria microwave during the defrosting process. She pulled the story from her backpack.

"Hey, stranger," she said as she approached.

He smiled. "Someone has to finish up the paper."

"You might have to change your address to the campus newsroom," Natalie said.

He shrugged and revealed a sheepish smile.

"But seriously, if you need help, don't hesitate to ask."

"It's cool. Mr. Moore's been in there every day at lunch, and a couple other staff writers."

"Right on." Paranoia crept up again. Up until now it seemed like he'd needed her help with the paper. Why was he turning down her offers? Was he avoiding more uncomfortable conversations about his best friend? She wished more than ever that she could rewind and take her words back. "That burrito looks like it took a brutal zap." She tried to keep things light.

He chuckled. "That's what I get for coming to lunch late. They were out of all the good stuff."

"What's in there, anyway?"

"Mystery meat and bean slop. You want a bite?" He held up the burrito.

"Sounds appetizing, but I think I'll pass this time."

She sat in the shade next to him. "Anyway," she said, "I loved your story."

"Really? You loved it?" He seemed self-conscious in a cute way, like he'd been a little uncertain and her praise had boosted his confidence.

"I thought it was awesome."

His smile grew wider as she shared her thoughts.

"It kept me up until four in the morning. Don't tell anyone, but I had to watch back-to-back episodes of *The Smurfs* just to come down from the fear."

"You're so funny, Nat," he said. She loved hearing him laugh.

"Seriously, you should write horror, Matt. I could see your name on the cover of a horror novel. It's really *that* good. I didn't have many notes. Just small things—things that maybe didn't make sense or typos."

"Cool." He smiled. "I can't wait to read your comments. So you think it's good enough for the paper?"

"Good enough for the paper? C'mon. It's almost too good for our little school newspaper."

The bell rang and everyone began to scatter in various directions, gathering their backpacks and saying good-bye to friends. Matt thanked her again for reading the story before Brianna met up with them. It had become routine for Natalie and Brianna to head to their classes together after lunch. She sort of wished she had a few more minutes to chat with Matt.

The girls said good-bye to Matt before leaving the cafeteria.

"Have you figured out what you're going as to the Howl at the Moon dance yet?" Brianna asked. "All the good stuff is selling out at the shop."

Ever since Jeremy and Natalie's initial visit to the costume shop, they'd sort of neglected searching for costumes. It had been a lingering source of dread for Natalie. Truthfully, it seemed like Jeremy wasn't as excited about finding costumes as he'd been in the past either. She assumed he probably had more important things to think about with his family problems and everything.

"We're not sure yet." Natalie wasn't in the mood to discuss costume ideas and decided to turn the focus to her new friend.

She knew Brianna didn't have a date to the dance, but figured it wouldn't be long before she found one. Pretty and cool, she had it all going for her. One of Jeremy's friends would snatch her up in no time. Or maybe Brianna just needed to make the first move. It seemed like Jeremy's baseball buddy Travis had his eye on her. Natalie often spotted them chatting during lunch.

"Why don't you ask someone to the dance?" Natalie asked. "You know this dance goes either way—girls can ask guys too. I can think of tons of Jeremy's friends you could go with. We'll find you a date."

"Well, actually I do have someone in mind."

"Really?" Natalie was excited for her. "That's great."

"Yeah, but I'm not sure if he already has a date. Maybe you know if he does. But if I tell you, you have to promise not to say anything."

It had to be Travis. Everyone knew that

they were flirting, and Travis was a good guy—he needed a date. "I'm almost positive Travis doesn't have a date yet," Natalie said. "I haven't heard of anyone asking him."

"Actually . . . I was thinking of asking Matt!"

"Matt? Matt. What a . . . fine choice. Good!" She'd never thought that Brianna would want to ask Matt to the dance, but it all made perfect sense now. When Matt was around during lunch, she had noticed them talking quite a bit. And how could she have ignored the giddy smile on Brianna only a few minutes ago when they had said good-bye to him.

Natalie wasn't supposed to feel disappointed by Brianna's choice. Brianna and Matt seemed like a perfect and obvious match. They were both down-to-earth and fun and likable. Why wouldn't she want to ask him? Natalie knew she would be acting like a total idiot if she was anything but encouraging. "He doesn't have a date. You should definitely ask him."

A million thoughts ran through her head—a million thoughts that she hated. She tried to remember that she'd be an idiot not to be happy for them. She had no right to feel anything other than hopeful for her two friends. But what if they fell madly in love? What if Natalie had to hang out with them all the time, and all the while her feelings for Matt grew deeper and deeper? What was her problem? She had a boyfriend. She wasn't free to pursue Matt, and even if she was, he didn't want her anyway. He thought she was great with Jeremy. Furthermore, Brianna was more than free. The thought of anyone asking him, and of Matt riding off into the Halloween sunset or full moon or whatever was appropriate for the dance, shouldn't feel unsettling to her, but it did.

She wasn't the type of person who could go for her boyfriend's best friend. She just wasn't, and though she wanted to believe that happy endings did exist, she knew they didn't. Look at the movie *Becoming Jane*. Jane Austen could've chosen to be with the man she loved. The consequence of choosing this particular guy would've let down everyone else in her life. Instead, she'd chosen the sensible path. This was a true story. Jane Austen had only written about all the happy endings in her books—in her works of fiction. Her real love life had ended sadly. That was life.

★

With all her obligations at the paper and her worries over her screwed-up love life, she hadn't even had much time to pursue her favorite indulgence—Romeohelpme. That night, she returned to her little world of escape and was excited to see that her cyber friends had been writing even when she wasn't around. She had tons of messages from all the usuals.

Where are you?
Member: Dragon Guy
Advanced Member
    Up All Night? What's up? Are you in the Witness Protection Program?

Member: Glamour Girl
Advanced Member
RE: Where are you?
    No kidding.

Member: Skater Chick
Newbie
RE: Where are you?
    It sure is boring around here.

She liked her cyber friends, and she felt as though she knew most of them even though she'd never seen them. She didn't even know their names. The only thing she knew of them were the voices she heard from their writing.

She was dying to talk to someone. She hadn't even told Jo or Vincent about all her true feelings. They knew she had doubts about Jeremy but they didn't realize how deep all these doubts went. She needed advice. Maybe she should just come clean. Spill everything to these nameless, faceless friends. There couldn't be a safer place to tell all. No one knew who she was. She began to type, and releasing her saga in words felt wonderful. Even if she ended up hitting delete, she'd still feel better. She just needed to get it out.

Writing her feelings reminded her of the time she was unfairly grounded for throwing a tennis ball through the laundry room window. It had been in retaliation for being attacked with Super Soak 'Em water guns from Thomas and Brandon. The tennis ball had been self-defense and was meant to drive them away. After being put on restriction for a weekend, she'd written her parents a very angry letter, citing in detail all their faults. It felt wonderful to get it all out, but in the end she'd torn up the letter.

She spent a long time spilling to her anonymous friends. She read her entry several times—changing words here, changing words there—until her eyes felt heavy and the clock read one a.m. She took a look at her final draft, uncertain as to whether or not she would even post it.

A huge dilemma
Member: Up All Night
Advanced Member

Hey, everyone. Sorry if I sort of disappeared for a few days there. I've been swamped with school and other worries. The truth is, my love life has been a complete disaster lately. Maybe you guys can help me out with a little advice. I just hope that after you all read this you don't think I'm a bad person. You see, I really like someone. I can't help it. I find myself thinking about him all the time and wondering what he's doing. I get butterflies when he's around, and I could spend hours talking to him. I've never felt such a connection with someone before. I don't think there is anyone else like him out there.

The only problem is that I have a

boyfriend. Oh, and did I mention that the guy I like is my boyfriend's best friend? You probably think I'm a horrible person, but I can't help the way I feel. If I could help it, I wouldn't like this person. Life would be so much easier.

You're probably asking why I don't just break up with this boyfriend of mine instead of stringing him along while pining over his best friend. Well, I can't break up with him. It would be cruel and unusual. He has a number of problems right now, and he's really turned to me during this hard time in his life. Breaking up with him at this point would be kicking him when he's down. I've gone over all the options in my head. One is to ask my parents for a pass to boarding school. I would never have to deal with any of this. The other is to do nothing and just accept that this is the cruel hand I've been dealt—similar to a Shakespearean tragedy. If anyone has other options, I would greatly appreciate hearing them.

Every time she read her posts on Romeohelpme, it was the same. She felt the same weirdness. She'd never get over the irony that this confused girl known as Up

All Night was the same one behind Coyote Courtship.

She looked at the growing pile of dirty laundry in her room. Two weeks' worth of clothes poured from her closet. Unless she wanted to smell like a linebacker after a football game in September, she was going to have to throw a load in the wash. She gathered up some clothes and headed downstairs. Except for the howling wind outside, her house was dead quiet. Everyone had gone to bed. She'd always found windy nights to be the eeriest. In San Diego the hot autumn winds could get violent, and with the threat of fires the sound was unsettling. Wind howled through cracks in the windows and everything outside rattled and shook. After she returned from the laundry room she checked her post. She waited an hour, checking text messages and raiding her pantry for snacks in the meantime. Her options at half past midnight were limited. She ended up with a bag of Doritos and a glass of orange juice.

She headed back upstairs, hoping some of her night owl friends would've responded by now. Disappointment hit heavily when her post showed no replies. Usually she had one or two by this time. Was everyone mad at her? Did they think she was a total nut for liking her boyfriend's best friend? Her situation couldn't get much worse. Not only had she driven Matt away, but now people she didn't even know thought she was crazy too. She hit refresh and the screen took her to a whole new page with some technical message. Great, now her computer wasn't working. She'd have her brother look at it tomorrow. She flopped onto her bed, buried her face in her pillow, and realized that she'd gone too far.

Thirteen

The wind woke Natalie. It blew so hard that something in the front yard slammed angrily against the garage door. The first thing she thought of was Romeohelpme and the fact that she was officially a cyber outcast. Then she realized that it was light outside. She glanced at her alarm clock. The numbers on the front flashed two a.m. The clock was out of commission. She grabbed her cell phone. *Six forty-five!* Panic washed her senses as she realized that she was late. Her alarm clock had never gone off. She was usually en route to school by this time. She wasn't even dressed. Worst of all, she wouldn't have time to peek to see if she had any replies. She'd have to wait until after school, which really meant dinnertime because she was supposed to study with Jo in the library today.

Typical that her alarm would fail the same day that she was horribly behind on laundry. She raced to the dryer for clean clothes. But when she opened the dryer door, all her clothes were heaped in a damp pile in the bottom.

Her mother peeked into the laundry room. "Oh good, you're up," she said. Natalie noticed that her hair was still wet. Usually her mother was blow-dried and ready to start the day by this point. "I was just about to go wake you. The power went out last night. The Santa Ana winds blew out the electricity."

"Does this mean the school's power is out too?"

Her mother shook her head. "I don't think so. Everything seems to be working now. I guess it blew out the whole south part of town earlier in the evening and eventually it got our power lines too. Listen, I have to run." She glanced at her watch and said good-bye.

Natalie mumbled something about being late before she rushed back upstairs.

In spite of her haste, she felt a huge sense of relief. The blackout explained the lack of replies. Her cable must've been screwed up before the electricity went out, thus messing up the Internet and not giving her updated posts.

She had no clean socks or jeans. She tore through her dresser looking for her khakis, but the only available pants were her sweatpants. Worse, she'd have to wear flip-flops. She couldn't find a T-shirt to match her loungewear so she dug frantically through her laundry basket sniffing things that looked clean. Everything was wrinkled and smelled like dirty clothes. She ended up in a hideous sweatshirt Grandma Jones had given to her for her birthday that read I LOVE DACHSHUNDS and had a picture of the breed on the front. She'd vowed she would never leave the house in the sweatshirt, but she was desperate. It was a terrible look. She'd only encountered bad laundry days a couple of other times in her life, and they always made for the most awkward of days. She'd feel weird and self-conscious all day, and she'd constantly want to explain her ugly ensemble to every person she encountered. *Sorry for my appearance. My alarm failed and*

I was too lazy to do laundry until I was out of clean underwear and socks.

To add to her bad start, her mother was long gone, so now she didn't have a note to excuse her from detention.

Spaces were limited in the Outer Space parking lot. She screeched into one in the farthest corner of the lot. The bell rang before she was even close to class. Several other students darted through the halls— some with wet hair and wrinkled clothes. At least she wasn't totally alone. The worst was walking into class in the middle of roll call in her terrible outfit. She felt every set of eyes focus on her. She'd never felt happier to duck into her assigned seat. After roll was finished, a detention slip followed. She hated the thought of detention and thought that a county-wide blackout was a perfectly good reason to get out of it. Wasn't the entire town of Oak Canyon affected?

"Everyone else managed to make it on time," her lame-o teacher pointed out. She couldn't stand Ms. Lizt. Natalie just knew the woman made a conscious effort to make her lectures as boring as possible and found joy in assigning homework.

Natalie ducked in and out of her classes

all day, finding the most comfort tucked behind her desk where she could hide better. At lunch she found Jo wearing a black dress she'd worn to her sister's graduation the year before and a hooded sweatshirt. She glanced at Natalie. "Looks like you had a bad laundry day too."

"You too?"

"I tried to do laundry last night but the freaking power went out."

"Same with me!" They compared bad outfits.

"I think your outfit is fine," Jeremy said. "What's wrong with it? I didn't even notice anything until you said something." He shrugged. She appreciated his words, but this was coming from someone who wore board shorts to school in December. Guys could get away with those sorts of things.

The afternoon moved slowly and Natalie couldn't wait to go home and finish up her laundry and check replies. However, she still had plans to meet with Jo in the library.

The girls met at their lockers after school and headed to the library together.

The library always smelled a little dusty—like old books. At least being here would force her to study and not procrastinate. They had both agreed that studying at Jo's house was a bad idea and had come to the library instead. At Jo's house they would've watched MTV and browsed the *Us Weekly* magazine subscription that Jo's mother had graciously agreed to.

The library was a little crowded but with school a month and a half in, everyone was starting to face their first big tests of the year. Jo and Natalie weren't in any of the same classes but they both had tests in biology and history. They found a table in the corner and began to unload books from their backpacks.

Jo made a small stack in front of her. "So I talked Brianna out of asking Matt to the dance," she whispered.

Natalie's head spun toward her friend. "How'd you know she was going to ask Matt?" Natalie hadn't mentioned this to Jo, and she tried to keep her reaction to this news cool.

"She told me today at lunch. She was going to ask him, but he wasn't around."

"Why'd you talk her out of it?"

Jo gave Natalie the same look her mother would give her when Natalie was trying to weasel her way out of something. "C'mon,

Nat. It's beyond obvious that there is something between you and Matt. And I only want what is best for my friend."

"What?" Natalie was shell-shocked. How did she know? Furthermore, it had always seemed like Jo had thought that Jeremy was perfect for her. "That's so not . . . I don't even know . . ." For a moment she thought of words that might allow her to talk her way out of this. But it was Jo. They'd known each other since elementary school. She was the closest thing Natalie had ever had to a sister, and she knew there was no use in trying to lie. Natalie scrunched up her forehead. "You think it's beyond obvious?"

"Well, only because I know you. I've suspected something between the two of you ever since you took on that newspaper job—which, by the way, I know you're writing the column too. You don't have to admit that now. But whenever you're ready you can tell me. And in the meantime, I swear I won't tell anyone." She pulled a strand of hair behind her ear.

Natalie was speechless. She'd always sensed that Jo knew her well, but now she was starting to wonder if her best friend shared the same gift as Seto. Or maybe she was Nancy Drew? "What are you? Jo Drew?"

Jo smiled. "I guess you could just call it intuition. And the fact that you're my oldest friend in the world and I can read you like a book, Natalie."

A million thoughts raced through her head. It was great and everything that Jo knew her so well, but Natalie didn't feel comfortable with the notion that she could be read like a book—by anyone. She liked to think she was pretty poker-faced most of the time. "Do you think Jeremy has sensed this too?"

"No. Not at all. He's totally oblivious."

"What about Vincent? Does he notice this too? Does everyone know?"

"I think Vincent might know."

"What do you mean 'might'?"

"Well, he did sorta say something that day we tried on costumes."

Natalie buried her face in her hands for a moment, then looked at her friend. "What did he say?"

"He just thought he sensed something too."

Her voice was barely a whisper. "All right, tell me what you said to Brianna."

"I just told her that Travis would be a better bet for the dance. He'd make a fun date."

"That was it?"

"I might've told her that Matt had a crush on someone else."

"Jo!" A guy at the adjacent table turned his head, and Natalie returned to whispering. "You can't do that. She was okay with that? Is she asking Travis?"

"I don't know. But I swear, truthfully, she really didn't seem all that bummed out."

"Really?"

"No. She said she kind of liked someone else anyway and she just thought Matt was cool."

"Really? She doesn't like Matt that much?"

"It didn't seem like it."

"Listen, even if Matt did have a crush on me, I would never hurt Jeremy. Ever. There is no hope for Matt and me. He is totally free and Brianna is completely free to pursue him. Matt even encouraged me to stay with Jeremy."

Jo blew it off. "He's only doing that to protect himself. Natalie, haven't you noticed the way he looks at you?"

Natalie shook her head. "I can't even believe I'm having this conversation. It's like talking about running for president of the United States. The whole thing is so far out of the question. And he looks at everyone that way."

Jo eyed her skeptically. "I don't think I totally agree with you."

"Why the sudden change of heart? I thought you loved Jeremy?"

"I think that you and Jeremy were great together at one point, but I realize now what you're saying. You guys have grown apart. You're different. So why can't you have a shot with Matt?"

"Why? Because what if Jeremy doesn't feel like we've grown apart? He would be devastated. I mean, hello? It's only his best friend in the world. What would you think if I swooped in and went for Brian?"

Jo sighed. "There is no generic black-and-white answer for everything. Geez, for someone in charge of an advice column about love, you sure could use some advice yourself. Everyone's situation is different. There are different circumstances for each unique situation. Yes, right now, today, if you went for Brian I would be mad. But maybe I won't even like him next month, and then he's all yours. And besides, we're in high school. What? Just because someone likes someone else means they forever have a claim on that person?" Jo shook her head. "No, I don't think so. This is the time in our lives when we're supposed to be dating— not marking our territory for life."

Natalie thought for a moment. "Hmmm. I never thought of it that way. But do you really think things are that simple?"

Jo nodded. "Yes."

After she returned from the library, Natalie holed up in her room with a bag of chips and finally had a chance to check her message board responses.

Member: Dragon Guy
Advanced Member
RE: A huge dilemma
    This is so much better than *The Hills*. I love it. Don't ask me what to do. But let me know what happens. I definitely want the outcome of this one.

Natalie chuckled. She would've never pegged Dragon Guy as a *Hills* fan. But that was the beauty of the site. Everyone could be themselves. She didn't feel so funny about revealing her deepest secret now.

Member: Skater Chick
Newbie
RE: A huge dilemma

I kind of saw this coming from your other posts. Screw what everyone else thinks. You can't live your life for other people. Go for him.

Member: Girl Gone Green
Newbie
RE: A huge dilemma

I don't agree with Skater Chick at all. Where are your ethics, people? Don't you know that what goes around comes around? You can't just hurt people like that. It's so uncool. And what about loyalty?

Member: Skater Chick
Newbie
RE: A huge dilemma

So, what? You're supposed to worry about everyone else for the rest of your life? That is how people end up in terrible situations they don't want to be in.

Member: Girl Gone Green
Newbie
RE: A huge dilemma
    You have no morals, Skater Chick.

Member: Skater Chick
Newbie
RE: A huge dilemma
    At least I'm not a people-pleasing
doormat like you.

Natalie's eyes grew wide. She never meant to start an outrage on Romeohelpme. That wasn't the end of it. At least two dozen other people threw in their two cents as well. Her love life was like an election. People were completely divided. Some stood strongly with Girl Gone Green, and others were totally committed to Skater Chick's beliefs. They were all eager to share their opinions.

You would have to be heartless to ever go for your boyfriend's best friend.

I think all is fair in love and war. Follow your heart.

Overnight, her cry for advice had become a battleground. One minute Natalie found herself agreeing with the Skater camp, and

the next she completely understood the Girl*
Gone Green philosophy.

However, there was one response that
she found particularly interesting.

Member: Glamour Girl
Advanced Member
RE: A huge dilemma
   **Wow, that's a really hard situation
you're in. You know what I would do? I
would write to an advice column with a real
expert. This question is too hard for this
website. I have an advice column in my
school newspaper, and whoever is behind
the column always has the best advice. I've
actually written in a couple times when I've
been in hard situations, and this mystery
writer is the best. I guarantee you that he or
she would know what to do.**

An expert? Natalie laid her head next
to her keyboard and sighed. She was a lost
cause.

Fourteen

Detention was packed. It seemed kind of cruel and ridiculous that they were all assigned detention when there was a blackout. Detention wasn't a regular thing for her, but she knew the drill. She averaged a couple detentions each year. She knew that you took a seat and waited for Mr. Pryce to call your name. Mr. Pryce was the head of discipline at Natalie's school. In other words, he was the one you had to visit if you got in serious trouble. Fortunately, Natalie had never paid him an office visit, but she was always aware of his presence around campus. A tall man, he had squinty, hawklike eyes and a thick blond mustache. He rarely smiled, spoke, or laughed. Jeremy had seen him a couple times for skateboarding across the quad and other similar offenses and had always said if Mr. Pryce didn't work at Oak Canyon High, he would've been a cop.

Detention was located in the old drama building, so the layout was similar to a theater, only the seats had pullout trays on the arms that were used as desktops for homework.

Natalie was looking for a seat when she heard someone call her name. "Hey, Nat."

She instantly recognized Matt's voice and felt her heart skip a beat. He was sitting in the very back row, which was filling up quickly.

"Come sit up here," he called.

She took this as an excellent sign. Maybe he wasn't weird about their talk in the parking lot the other night.

By the time she made her way to the back row, there wasn't an available seat left.

"I'll move," he offered.

"It's okay. I can sit here." She pointed to the row in front of him—also filled.

"Nah, it's fine. I'll move." He began to gather his books.

They found seats next to each other several rows down. Natalie pulled out her desktop from the chair and plopped her backpack on top. In a way, detention came at a good time. She'd be forced to study instead of procrastinating.

"I have a rough layout of what the paper is going to look like this month. Do you want to see?" Matt asked.

"I'd love to," she said. "I'm sure it's far more interesting than the math test I have to study for."

As he reached into his backpack, the detention bell rang. Natalie knew this meant silence. "I'll show you after," Matt whispered.

If one was caught talking past the detention bell, the consequence was two more detentions.

She nodded.

Mr. Pryce took roll, then gave his mini lecture about the consequences of passing notes, text messaging, or basically doing anything other than schoolwork. Natalie opened her math book and stared at the pages. She needed to study but all she could think about was Denny's and how she felt like such a fool for choking and for spilling her guts. She was such a moron. She wondered if Matt was annoyed that she hadn't answered that question for the column. As she sat there dwelling, it hit her. Matt had written that question. It had to be him. When they'd been at Denny's, he'd said something about the question being a hard one to answer. The funny thing was, the question had been sealed and stamped in an envelope. How would he have known what the question was? He wrote it. Her heart started to race. She couldn't believe that she hadn't realized this before. But then again, she'd almost choked to death on a cheese fry. Her thoughts had been slightly preoccupied after her near-death experience and rescue from Helga the Heimlich Hero.

The detention bell buzzed her from her thoughts. Her fellow students poured from the detention hall as though a fire had started. Apparently, she hadn't been the only anxious one.

"You want to go grab a soda at the lake and I can show you the paper?" Matt offered.

"Sure," she said. She'd hardly had time to process her realization about the column. She felt sort of flustered. Had he been writing about her? It had to be about her. Who else did he know in a relationship?

Oak Canyon Lake was right around the corner from their school, and students sometimes went after school for sodas.

"I have to drive separately, though," he said. "I have to pick up my brother in about"—he glanced at his watch—"thirty minutes."

"Sure."

They drove separately to the lake, and when they arrived, it was pretty desolate. Natalie noticed a few men fishing, but other than that she didn't see anyone from Oak Canyon High School. The large lake backed up to a massive reservoir. A couple years ago the whole area had been surrounded by massive oak trees and shrubs. But fires had raged through the park during a nasty Santa Ana and had taken all the big trees with them. The area was green again but the hillsides were flat and young looking.

They ordered sodas from the snack shack, then headed to a quiet area next to the water. They perched themselves on a rock and Matt pulled out the paper.

He pointed to where her column would go and proofs of the artwork and photos for several other stories.

"I love the artwork for my quiz!" she

said. The newspaper's artist had drawn little sketches of her personality profiles. "My favorite is Dressed for Success. Look at how funny the doctor's face looks. He just looks like an overachiever!"

Matt agreed. "I thought those turned out really good too. The only thing that isn't finished is the cover," he said. "We're still not sure what's going on the front page."

"What about your story?"

He shrugged. He took the last sip of his soda, then set the empty can down next to him on the rock.

"I still haven't shown it to Mr. Moore yet."

"Matt! Why not?"

"I don't know."

"You need to show it to him. Today! It's so good. You're crazy if you don't show it to him."

He dug the tips of his shoes in the dirt beneath the rock. "You still feeling confused?"

The question had caught her off guard. She assumed he would never go there again.

He threw a pebble in the lake and it bounced over the water. Then he looked at her with his big blue eyes, and she felt like she was the only person in the world.

"Matt, it was you. Wasn't it?" Her heart raced as the words left her mouth. She hadn't planned on asking him. She'd hardly had time to absorb it. "You wrote in with that question, didn't you?"

Their eyes locked, and she felt a warmth surge up from her belly to meet her heart. Before she knew what was happening they were leaning toward each other. His lips felt warm and she wanted to be closer to him. He felt like the warmest being on earth. And then a moment of reality hit. She wasn't sure who pulled away first, but the kiss lasted no more than half a second before it felt like someone had shined a flashlight on them in the dark of night. This was so wrong.

"I am sorry," Matt said immediately. "That was totally not meant to happen."

"It's okay," she said. "I shouldn't have let that happen. That was terrible. I mean, not terrible. But the whole situation is just completely messed up. I feel awful."

"It was my fault, really."

He slid from the rock. Natalie followed.

"I'm gonna go," she said.

"That's a good idea. I'll walk you to your car."

"No. That's okay." She already stood a good ten feet from him when she turned down his suggestion. She felt as though she needed to move. It was like there was a fire between them, and if she didn't get out of there quickly, she was going to burn herself. "I'll be fine," she said. "Talk to you later."

He waved as she walked away. She thought about how stupid her words had been. Talk to you later? She'd just kissed the guy, and they both knew there would be no later. There was no hope for them. Matt's eyes were the last thing she noticed before she walked away, and she knew by looking into them that he was thinking the same exact thing.

Fifteen

"Call Jo," she barked at the phone. Due to the hands-free cell phone laws in California, her phone was programmed to a voice activation system. Her parents had set up this whole hands-free device in her car. The only thing she had to do was lock her cell phone into a little holder on the center console and then talk to it. She pulled out of the parking lot so fast that the Ravioli left skid marks.

Thank goodness her best friend answered quickly. "I just kissed Matt."

Jo screamed so loud that Natalie wondered if her hearing would ever be the same again. "Oh my God! What? How did it happen? Are you serious?" Then she lowered her voice. "Wait. Hang on. I have to go outside. Seto is staring at me. Vincent is here too. Do you care if he hears?"

"No," Natalie said. He already knew she had a crush on Matt, anyway. Vincent was a good one to hit up for advice during a crisis too.

Natalie could hear their feet tapping down the hardwood floors in Jo's house, then the sound of a door closing behind them. "Oh my God," Jo squealed. "I can't believe this. Now tell me everything. But wait! I'm putting you on speaker."

"Hi, Vinny," Nat said.

"So, let's hear the drama," he replied.

"It just happened," Natalie said. "One minute we were talking about the newspaper, and, it's a complicated story, but I figured out that it was him that had written in with this question and then . . ."

"Did he kiss you first?" Jo asked.

Vincent interjected before Natalie replied, and his comments were directed toward Jo. "Do you want to be Miss Jump Ahead? Is that what you're going to do? Be Miss Jump Ahead the whole story? Let's listen and give her a chance. Save questions until the end, please."

"Sorry," Jo said. "I'm just dying to hear what happened."

Natalie smiled in spite of her frazzled nerves. She continued. "I don't know what happened or who kissed who first, but we both leaned in and kissed. It was only for, like, two seconds. I think we were both freaked out because we both pulled away. And then things were so weird. I just wanted to get out of there instantly, and I think he did too. He said it should've never happened, and I agreed."

"How did you leave it?" Jo asked.

"I said I would talk to him later— whatever that's supposed to mean. You guys, I feel so bad. I don't know what came over me. I should've never let that happen. Poor Jeremy. I am such a horrible person."

"Okay, stop. Stop right now." It was Jo again. "Maybe it shouldn't have happened. But it did, and think about it . . . you guys couldn't help it."

"What do I do now? I don't want things to be weird between Matt and me. I just want to pretend like it never happened. The guilt is going to kill me. I'll never be able to sleep again."

"But it did happen," Jo said.

"Don't remind me." Her palms felt sweaty against the steering wheel, and she flipped on the air-conditioning.

"You guys can't deny it forever," Jo said. Natalie admired her romantic view of the future, but she just didn't think that Jo's outlook was realistic.

"It shouldn't have happened like this, though," Natalie said. "I should've broken up with Jeremy, then told him I had feelings for Matt. And I shouldn't even be telling you guys. I feel like I'm going behind his back with everything."

"I kind of see what you're saying," Vincent said.

"Yeah," Jo agreed, even though it went against all her romantic ideas.

The sound of Natalie's phone beeping startled her. "I have another call," she said.

"Who is it?" they both asked.

Natalie glanced at her phone. "Jeremy! I can't talk to him right now. But on the other hand, maybe I should just tell him. I should just come clean and get it over with."

"No!" Jo said. "Don't answer."

"Why?" The phone beeped again and Natalie knew she had about two seconds to click over before it would go to voice mail.

"Don't," Vincent warned. It was the first advice he'd given since she'd spilled the story, and Natalie felt like she should probably listen.

"This is not the way to do it. You're only going to hurt him. There has to be a better way to resolve this," Jo pointed out.

"Maybe I should just move. Maybe I should convince my parents we need to leave the state, and then I could avoid everything in this whole situation."

"C'mon."

"Well, do you have a better idea?"

Jo was quiet. "Honestly, not at the moment. But I know there has to be one."

"Vinny?"

"I have to think about this one," he said.

It was a strange response coming from him. Vincent always had the best advice. "But don't worry, Natty. I know you're going to drive yourself insane worrying."

"No, I won't."

Natalie stayed up most of the night worrying. She worried about Jeremy. She worried about Matt. She worried about the dance and the column. She didn't even want to confess to her cyber friends about the kiss. It

seemed too heavy a secret for even an anonymous website.

What was Matt thinking?

To relieve her stressed nerves, she jotted
down the possibilities on a notepad.

> A. He only wrote in with the
> question to test me and my
> skills as a columnist and
> now thinks I'm nuts for
> kissing him.
> B. He is equally worried and
> is debating telling Jeremy as
> soon as he can work up the
> nerve.
> C. He has hardly thought about
> it—chalked it up to poor
> judgment and is glued to a
> horror novel.

On one hand, she felt that they needed to
talk. On the other, it might be best if they
never spoke again. The kiss was enough, but
now calling him would be admitting the
kiss had actually occurred, and a cover-up
would be in the works. It just seemed so
sneaky. But something had to be said, just
so there wouldn't be any weirdness between

them. Jeremy's birthday was in two days, and they'd for sure cross paths at the bowling alley. Then there was still the newspaper. They had to keep things cool and casual. Otherwise, there would always be weird tension between them.

She knew one thing for certain. She needed to break up with Jeremy. It didn't matter if she had a chance with Matt or not. It wasn't fair to string Jeremy along when she had kissed his best friend. Obviously, Matt knew she didn't have feelings for Jeremy anymore, and the cool thing to do was to let Jeremy go in the nicest possible way. She couldn't do it before his birthday party, but she had to do it soon.

After everyone was asleep, she headed downstairs and watched TV in the dark. By three o'clock in the morning she finally fell asleep on the couch. She was awakened by the sound of cleats on the tile.

Her brothers entered in matching football uniforms, each holding a helmet.

"What are you doing?" Thomas asked.

"What time is it?" She answered him with a question.

"Eight thirty." Her father peered over their shoulders.

"Why did you sleep on the couch?" Brandon wanted to know.

"I was watching TV and I fell asleep."

"Jeremy called you on the home line last night," her father said. "He said you weren't answering your phone. So I told him you were asleep."

"Oh, thanks. I'll call him back. Thanks for telling me."

"When is Jeremy coming over again?" Thomas looked worried. Or maybe she was just paranoid.

"Do you think he can come to our game today?" Brandon asked.

"Yeah, that was fun when he came to our baseball games," Thomas reflected.

"I think he has plans," Natalie said, feeling even worse for lying to her family now.

"Everything okay?" her dad asked.

"Everything is fine."

After they left, Natalie could stand it no longer. She sent Matt a text.

I hope we're not weird about what happened yesterday. Let's just forget about the whole thing. I'm willing to erase. It was a huge mistake.

She meant it. At this point she just wanted to pretend as though it had never occurred—to erase the entire incident from her thoughts. She wouldn't hurt Jeremy. She'd still be friends with Matt. Life would go on.

She waited a few hours, checking her cell phone every ten seconds to see if he had replied. Nothing. She made a million excuses for him. *He'd lost his cell phone at the beach yesterday. Waves had taken it, and it was now lying at the bottom of the Pacific. His battery was dead. The charger had flown out his car window when he'd fled San Diego in an attempt to escape the situation. He'd moved; he'd decided it was the only option. He hated her and was horrified by the fact that she'd even be capable of doing something so sneaky to Jeremy.*

She still had to call Jeremy back. He'd called her home line? He never called the home line. Did he know? The guilt was almost too much to bear. But she knew if she avoided him it was only worse. Grandma Jones was lurking somewhere in the house, so Natalie sought privacy in her bedroom.

He answered on the first ring. "Hey, what's up with you?"

"I was so tired last night. I came home

from school and literally passed out. My dad just told me you called."

"I tried to call you and text you on your cell last night—a bunch of times."

"I'm sorry. I didn't know."

He was quiet for a moment. "Okay. Well, I'm going to the skate park. Maybe we can meet up later or something."

"Or for sure tomorrow. Tomorrow is your big day!" she said.

"It should be fun."

They said good-bye, and after she hung up with him she realized she still hadn't picked up a birthday gift. What was becoming of her life? One day she was kissing her boyfriend's best friend, and the next she was buying the same boyfriend birthday gifts? Who was she? She didn't want to be some sneaky diva.

She had to get out of the house. She met Jo for ice cream at Cold Stone. She'd wanted Vincent to join too, but he had to read lines for *South Pacific*. Natalie ordered chocolate ice cream with a Rocky Road blend of nuts and marshmallows. She also had them throw in some peanut butter cup chips for an extra sugar fix. Jo always scrunched up her nose when Natalie ordered. They had completely different tastes when it came to ice cream. Jo opted for the fruity flavors while Natalie liked the rich, creamy ones. As Jo ordered her strawberry shortcake concoction, Natalie thought she saw another personality quiz brewing. *What does your favorite flavor of ice cream say about you?* She liked quizzes, and maybe it would even give her an excuse to talk to Matt.

They found a table outside, and as soon as they were settled Natalie looked over her shoulder. Call it paranoia, but she didn't want anyone from their school overhearing their discussion about her soap opera love life.

As soon as she felt comfortable, she ran every excuse from the list she'd made the night before by Jo.

Jo tossed her a look. "First of all, he wasn't *testing* you. I mean, didn't he kiss you back? And he wrote in with that question. It had to be him."

Natalie thought for a moment. "Well, yes. He did kiss me back. But what if he didn't write in with the question? He never answered me before we kissed. And I've thought about this some more. Matt wouldn't stamp the envelope with a

Spider-Man stamp. That's so weird. That's so not him."

"He has a little sister, though. Maybe it was her stamp and he just wanted to make sure no one opened it. It actually sounds a lot like Matt. It's pretty smart if you think about it. The stamp makes it look even more like it wasn't him—like you'd never guess him. He was just being careful. And give him some time to reply to your text. It's only been three hours!"

"Four and a half now."

"Well, just wait till tomorrow. No, Monday. If you haven't heard from him by Monday, then we can start analyzing."

"Really, I think the only reason he hasn't replied is because he just doesn't want to talk to me. That's the reality. And I can't wait until Monday because I'm going to see him tomorrow at Jeremy's party." Natalie shook her head. "This is horrible. What kind of person am I? Throwing a party for my boyfriend while worrying about kissing his best friend. I'll never get over the guilt. Not to mention how awkward it's going to be at the bowling alley."

Jo pushed around a strawberry in her sweet cream ice cream. "I'll be there too.

And Vincent. So maybe that can keep you away from some of the awkwardness."

Natalie decided to change the subject. There was no sense in driving herself crazy with worry, or driving Jo crazy with her incessant worrying. Furthermore, she felt a little selfish for focusing so much on herself and all her love life problems. They hadn't even talked about Jo's life in two days.

"Did Vinny find a suit for the dance?" Natalie asked.

Jo nodded vigorously as she swallowed her ice cream. "He did. It's so perfect. We drove down to the vintage shops in Pacific Beach and found the coolest suit. Then Vincent took it home and put it in cold water and hung it outside to dry. So it's all stiff. It looks like it came straight out of a grave. We're going to put little fragments of spiderweb and dust on it too. It's going to be so gothic chic. I'm actually kind of excited to go to the dance with Vincent again this year. We always have the best time picking out costumes."

"You guys have the best time doing everything. I don't know why you don't give the guy a fair chance." Natalie licked the back of her spoon.

"I don't know."

"What don't you know?"

"I mean, he's like a brother. And I just don't think I'm attracted to him that way."

Of all people Natalie should understand. Feelings were feelings. If that's the way Jo felt, she couldn't help it. Even if it seemed like such romantic injustice.

"Did I tell you that you guys both scored the same way on the quiz?"

Jo shook her head. "No."

"You guys both got 'dressed to dream.' See, you're perfect for each other, and how many guys are romantic that way? He'd be such a good boyfriend."

"The truth is, I think about him all the time. I know he would be. But it just seems so weird. I just don't know." She thought for a moment, then shook her head. "No, I just can't see it happening."

Natalie had to make one more point. "Look, I'm not saying you have to marry the guy. But why don't you just give him a chance? You even said so yourself. Now is the time for dating. It's just a time to test the waters."

Jo didn't argue. Maybe there was hope.

Sixteen

Natalie stomped her foot in exasperation as she watched her ball roll into the gutter for the third time. "Where's your form?" Jeremy called, half joking.

She smiled and shook her head.

Bowling ball in hand, Jo passed her on the way to the lane. "Nice try, Nat."

Jo was smoking the guys, and Natalie wished she could say the same for herself.

She was terrible at bowling. There was no other way to put it. She needed the smallest and lightest ball the alley offered, and she had to roll the ball from in between her calves using both hands—a technique Jeremy referred to as "granny style." However, in spite of all this she still thought the sport was pretty fun. It wasn't like everyone expected her to be some champion bowler. A dozen of Jeremy's friends had shown up for the party, and most of them had probably only bowled a handful of times in their lives. Jeremy had a natural flair for bowling, but that came as no surprise. When it came to sports he was good at everything he tried. Jo had surprised Natalie the most. Natalie had never expected Jo to bowl better than Jeremy. For some strange reason, Jo just seemed to have a knack for it. The rest of the party fell somewhere in between Jo and Natalie, so Natalie wasn't alone in her defeat.

Natalie also loved the people-watching at the bowling alley. The lane on the left hosted a birthday party for a twelve-year-old, and all the guests had come in costume. It was pretty funny watching Pocahontas get a strike or Cinderella roll the ball granny style as Natalie had been doing all afternoon.

The lane on the right was another story. It was an older group. Natalie guessed they were in their twenties. Most were dressed from head to toe in black, and the dark eye makeup and onyx nail polish worn by the girls and guys brought visions of Marilyn Manson concerts. It wasn't every day she saw a bunch of goths bowling, and she would've never pinned them as the bowling type. She would've thought séances and AFI concerts were more their thing.

But no matter how different everyone was in their costumes or their dark attire, they all wore the same shoes. Natalie observed that bowling shoes didn't look bad on anyone.

She watched Jeremy bowl a strike. He did a victory dance before Brianna took her turn at the lane. She came close to a strike, and then managed to wipe out the next pins on the following try. Brianna jumped up and Travis gave her a high five on his way to the lane. She still hadn't asked him to the dance, and Natalie made a mental note to bring it up if she had a chance later in the party.

"That was awesome," Jeremy said as she returned to their party beaming. They high-fived.

Then it was Vincent's turn. He was a bad bowler too. He looked kind of funny when he rolled the ball. His legs sort of caved in at the knees, almost as though they were going to collapse, and his arm jutted out to the side.

"Keep your arm in," Jeremy yelled.

The comment must've distracted Vincent because his ball took off at a grotesquely odd angle. Natalie watched as his ball bounced off the side of the gutter and landed in the goths' lane. She'd hoped the ball would keep heading east and only cause a moment of interruption for their warlock neighbors. Instead, the ball rapidly headed south.

Natalie caught a glimpse of Vincent's eyes growing wide. He mumbled something that would've been bleeped out on TV before his ball took out a few pins on the left side of the goths' lane. She hoped whoever's turn it was in the vampire clan was bowling as badly as Vincent was because this could either make their game or totally ruin it.

The only person who seemed to find this funny was Jeremy. Everyone else in their group wore the same *oh no* expressions. Jeremy's laughter bounced off the alley's walls and could probably be heard down the street. He doubled over. "That is freaking hilarious," he said in between breaths. His baseball cap fell off and he caught it.

"Sorry," Vincent called. "I'm sure you can remove it from your score." He lowered his voice and looked at Jo and Nat. "I just have no idea how."

Surprisingly, the Marilyn Manson crew cracked a few smiles. "No worries," one of the goths called back. "It was Karen's turn, and she needed the points anyway."

"Great! Glad I could help," Vincent said as he quickly returned to the party. He slid into a seat next to Natalie. "Okay, that should make you feel better," he said.

She laughed.

"One of us has to be the worst and I think it might be me," he said.

"Actually, in spite of your lane invasion I think you're still beating me." She glanced at the scoreboard. "Yep, you are."

"Where's Matt?" Vincent whispered.

Natalie shrugged. The question had been eating away at her since the party had started an hour ago. It was so not like him to be a no-show. Avoiding her text message from the day before was one thing. But now he blew off Jeremy's birthday party? Maybe he really had fled the country.

"Has Jeremy said anything about where he is?" Vincent's voice was almost inaudible.

She shook her head.

"Why don't you ask him?"

"I will." Natalie didn't know why she felt as though she needed to work up the nerve to ask Jeremy where Matt was. It seemed as though even speaking his name indicated guilt. She felt like waiting. Maybe he would still show up. After all, bowling had been his idea. It was just so not him to avoid his best friend's birthday, no matter how weird he felt.

The other thing that had been holding her back from asking was that Jeremy hadn't sat still for more than two seconds. If she wanted to know where Matt was, she was going to have to yell over the group. But even with their friends she felt weird bringing Matt up. Was everyone going to point in her direction and accusingly say, "You! You kissed him."

She realized how irrational and weird she was being. She waited until Jeremy was nearby. He was chatting with Brianna, and Natalie tapped the back of his leg with her bowling shoe.

"So, where's Matt?" she asked after he faced her.

"Oh, did I forget to tell you? He's sick. He called me this morning. He sounds like a freaking chain-smoker. I hardly recognized him."

"Oh."

He quickly turned back to Brianna.

Natalie was glad she'd asked. But then she wondered if she would get what he had. What if she sounded like a chain-smoker tomorrow? How much more guilty could she look? It would be the wrath of God.

Natalie came in dead last, and Jo and Jeremy tied for first place. Natalie wondered what Jeremy would've done if Jo had beat him. He'd probably demand another game. They sang "Happy Birthday" and ate the chocolate cake that Natalie had picked up from the grocery store. Several people brought gifts and they all watched while Jeremy opened them. In the past Natalie's gifts to Jeremy had had sentimental value or had been something special she knew that he'd wanted. This time she'd picked up an an iTunes gift card from the grocery store when she'd picked up the cake. He seemed happy with the gift.

The party came to a close and Jo and Vincent stayed to help clean up. Natalie drove Jeremy and his gifts home. For the entire ride home he blasted the new Slipknot CD that Brianna got him. After one song, Natalie was ready to chuck it out her window and watch it shatter into twenty million pieces. She'd rather hear the ravioli song.

"Thanks for the party, Nat. This was great."

"You're welcome. Did you have fun?"

"I had a blast."

"Don't forget this." She ejected his CD.

"Oh yeah." He took the CD and she helped him carry the rest of his gifts to the front door. His mother had decorated their porch with a scarecrow. The head was lopsided, a detail that Jeremy quickly pointed out. Rather than fixing the head, he pushed it with his free hand and watched as it rolled down the porch steps. So Jeremy.

He chuckled as he looked for Natalie's reaction. She smiled and rolled her eyes. "Real nice."

"It was begging to be beheaded," he said.

They said good-bye in his foyer, and as she walked back to her car, she realized it was the first time that they had ever parted ways without a kiss.

Seventeen

The party was over, in many ways.

Matt didn't show up to school on Monday. She was sort of glad. After a lot of thinking she realized that it was probably best if she didn't see him until after she broke up with Jeremy. Maybe the fact that they'd be officially broken up the next time she saw Matt would make things seem less sneaky and scandalous.

She'd spent most of Sunday night and Monday thinking of an easy way to let Jeremy go. She thought about asking her cyber friends, but she had Jo and Vincent to confide in now, and she trusted them more than anyone. Furthermore, she didn't want to start another war on Romeohelpme. Her last entry had drawn in more visitors than she'd ever imagined. Everyone had an opinion about her dilemma. She thought it was best to lie low on Up All Night until the situation was resolved and she could think a little more clearly.

The hardest part was that she had decided to tell Jeremy everything—even about kissing Matt. Even her best friends had conflicting opinions on this particular dilemma. Jo thought she should come clean and Vincent had advised against it.

"He's going to find out eventually," Jo had said a thousand times. "It would be best if he found out from you. And it's the right thing to do."

"Maybe come clean down the road," Vincent said. "When things aren't so raw. But don't let the guy lose his girlfriend and best friend all in one day."

She realized there was never going to be the perfect answer for this. So she had to do what she felt was best, in her heart. The more she thought about it, the more she knew she wouldn't be able to live with herself if she kept such a huge secret from him.

She'd never broken up with anyone in her life. It was hard enough thinking that her decision was going to be the source of someone else's pain. She wasn't even sure about what she should say. She'd been searching for the right words all day.

After school she got in her car and thought of different options, and wanted to call her friends for one more chat. She reached in her backpack for her cell phone. While steering, she didn't have a chance to place it in its holder. She held on to the phone and waited for a red light so she could get situated.

She tried to think of the right thing to say. *I just need a break—just some time to find out if this is right. I still want you in my life, and I will always be here for you. It's not you. It's me. You're wonderful. And there is something else I need to tell you. I kissed Matt.*

No matter how lightly she put it, the message was still the same. It was over. It was going to hurt. Her September column had been devoted to breaking up, but she'd never realized how hard it was until she was actually in that position.

She had that song by Fergie about breaking up stuck in her head all day. "It's not you, it's me" was basically the message. It wasn't her favorite song, but Fergie had really hit the nail on the head. It was nothing personal. Natalie just needed some time to figure things out. Natalie nervously ran her fingers through her hair while still holding her cell phone. Wouldn't it be nice if she could put things as easily as Fergie had?

The sound of a siren interrupted her thoughts. The moment she heard the noise was the same moment she realized that she'd been singing out loud. She looked at her hands and realized she'd been holding the cell phone the entire time too. The officer thought that she'd been talking on her cell phone. She'd been singing! She tossed her cell phone on the Ravioli's passenger seat and pulled over. She'd never been pulled over in her entire life. She'd only witnessed her father getting a speeding ticket once.

Panic-stricken, she maneuvered the car to the side of the road. Cars whizzed past her as she waited for the officer to arrive at her window. She recognized many of her class-mates' cars as they sped past her. She even heard someone scream "Hi, Naaaaaaaaaaaat!" from his window.

She noticed Jo's car head past, and Vinny was looking out the window pointing at her. This was just her luck.

How was she going to explain that she was singing—not talking on her cell phone? She'd never even heard of someone getting a ticket for singing. Jo had gotten one of those red-light tickets—the kind where the camera snaps a photo of you running a red light, and then the police department mails the picture and the fine to you. Jo had been singing in the photograph. But this was different—Natalie was seriously getting pulled over for belting out the lyrics to some lame breakup song. What were her parents going to say?

The cop looked even more intimidating up close. Was it a rule that cops had to have mustaches? He had thick lips and chubby, porklike fingers. Freckles covered his obscenely pale complexion.

"You know why I'm pulling you over?" he asked.

"Let me explain for a minute here. Officer, I swear I was putting my cell phone in the holder, and I just couldn't reach while I was driving. I was actually waiting for a light to snap my cell phone into the charger—trying to be safe—and, and I was singing. I swear, I really truly was singing."

His chuckle was sinister. "That's a new

one. Haven't heard that one before. But it's a good one." He began to write her a ticket.

"I'm serious! I mean, look. I have a hands-free device right here in my car." She pointed to the holder. "Why would I talk on my phone when I have that? Why? No one would do that. No one in their right mind."

He looked up from his ticket pad. "What were you singing?"

He wanted to know? She wasn't about to question why. "I was singing that Fergie song. I can't remember the name of it." She was feeling desperate and began to sing the chorus to him. She couldn't see his eyes behind his cop shades, but she sensed he was enjoying her performance. "You recognize it?" she asked.

He shook his head. "Sorry. No." Then he ripped the ticket from the pad.

"You're really giving me a ticket?"

"'Fraid so." He tapped the side of her car. "Be careful out there."

She looked in her rearview mirror and watched him shake his head with laughter all the way back to his squad car.

Her phone beeped, indicating the arrival

of a text. However, she wasn't about to touch the thing at this point. She'd probably get arrested.

Pulling away from the curb was terrifying. She worried about getting in an accident right there with the cop watching her. Or worse, getting in an accident *with* the cop. Was she supposed to go first? Or wait for him to leave? He went first, speeding away with his siren on. She waited for a long time, just to let her nerves cool off.

When she arrived home, there was a note on the banister from her mother.

Natalie,
The boys had football practice today. And I took Grandma to get her hair cut. I'm bringing dinner home.
Love,
Mom

Perfect. She wasn't looking forward to explaining to her parents that she'd been pulled over for singing. What if they didn't believe her?

Even though no one was home, she went

to her room and closed the door behind her. She checked her texts.

Vinny.

R U OK?

She had another from Jeremy.

Did someone have a run-in with Johnny Law? What were u doing?

Had the entire school seen her?

She called Jo and Vincent first. Both of them almost died laughing when they heard her story.

"That might be one of the best stories I've ever heard in my life," Jo said.

Vincent began singing the Fergie song. "I like that song," he said.

"Anyway," Natalie said, changing the subject, "I have to call Jeremy."

They both already knew she had plans for "a big talk" with him, but refrained from asking her a lot of questions. She appreciated their consideration. It was only fair to go to Jeremy first.

She said good-bye to her friends, then waited for a moment. She was nervous. In fact, she couldn't recall ever being more nervous. She'd felt more confident about the speech she had given on economics last year. She'd gotten through the speech, and she told herself she'd get through this, too. She might even feel better when it was over.

Her heart pounded as she dialed Jeremy. He answered quickly. Right off the bat he wanted to know about the ticket.

"You all right?" he asked.

She told him the whole story, and he also burst into hysterics. "That's pretty funny," he said.

"Only me, right?"

He asked her a million questions about the experience, and she waited until he was finished to bring up the main reason for her phone call.

Her heart skipped a beat. "Anyway, I'm also calling because . . . I think we need to talk." She paused. "In person."

"O-kay," he said slowly. "About what?" She sensed from his serious tone that he knew the answer. He sounded worried, so unlike himself.

"Just about stuff . . ." Now she sounded nervous. "Specifically you and me."

He wanted to meet at the lake, which

wasn't her first choice after what had happened there only days ago. But she was afraid her father would come home and then she wouldn't be able to break up with him. And they couldn't go to his house because his mom and brother were there. Any crowded public places were out of the question. At least at the lake they could find their own secluded area to chat.

They agreed to meet at the lake in fifteen minutes. She was glad they didn't delay it because she needed to get this over with. She'd finally worked up the nerve, and if she waited too long, she might change her mind. He was standing at the water's edge when she arrived, throwing rocks into the lake and watching them bounce off the water. He hardly noticed her walk up.

"Hey, Jere," she said.

He turned around, and the happy-go-lucky look he usually greeted her with was gone. The only other time he'd been like this was when he'd told her about his parents splitting up. He hugged her, which she took as a good sign. At least he didn't hate her—yet. But the hug seemed more like a good-bye than a hello. He totally knew what was coming, and she felt horrible. She almost changed her mind about breaking up with him. She couldn't stand to see him suffer. However, it was worse to stay with him out of pity.

"Let's sit down," he said.

She sat down next to him in the sand. For a moment he continued picking up small rocks and throwing them in the water.

"Natalie," he started, then paused.

"I'm sorry, Jeremy," she said. "I don't think I've been completely honest with you. There is a lot I want to say, and there is just no easy way to say it." She swallowed, then took a deep breath. Here it was. "I think we've grown apart, Jere. I love you as a friend, and I never want to lose that. I mean, I would die if I lost you as a friend, but—"

"No, hey, listen. It's my fault." He held on to a rock, making a fist around its smooth surface.

"What's your fault?"

"That we've grown apart."

She was shocked. All this time, she'd assumed he thought they were closer than ever. All his confiding and late-night chats. She felt as though a weight had been lifted off her back.

"We're great friends," he continued. "I

think that in many ways our friendship is closer than ever. I mean, I really care about you. But I think . . ."

"The spark is gone?"

He nodded.

"You don't have to explain. I completely understand."

He seemed relieved too.

"I still really want to be friends with you, and you know you can always come to me for anything," she emphasized.

"That's good. Because you've probably been the closest friend that I've had this past year." Instead of throwing the rock that he held into the lake, he set it down next to him.

"Thanks for saying that. You really deserve someone better than me, Jeremy."

"That's not true. I think you deserve better than me."

They sat next to the lake for a while. It was starting to feel more like fall had finally arrived in San Diego. The breeze felt cool off the lake, and the sun seemed to cast different shadows than it had in the summer—as though it were getting darker earlier.

Natalie had thought breaking up would put a heavy tension between the two of them, and in many ways it was sad, but the strange thing was that everything felt lighter, more relaxed. But she still had to tell him about Matt. Dread consumed her. But she was afraid that this amicable breakup might turn ugly. Then she thought about the dance.

"What about the dance?" she asked.

"Do you still want to go?"

She didn't want to hurt his feelings— what if he still really wanted to go?—and it was a little late to find a date at this point. "I'm definitely still in if you're still in. But I don't mind either way."

"You want to just swing it solo this year?"

"Sure."

He thought for a moment. "But what about the nominations?"

"Jo's on the committee. I'm sure she can take us off the ballot. You know the votes aren't cast until the night of the dance anyway."

He nodded. "I hope it's not too much of a problem."

"Seeing how we don't even have costumes yet, I think we're okay."

He smiled. "True." He looked at the lake. "Well, if you don't want to go, do you care if I ask Brianna?"

She was surprised—not in a bad way. She just hadn't seen that one coming.

She shook her head. "Not at all."

It was a relief to know that he already had his eye on someone else. Brianna wasn't her best friend, though. At the end of the day, Matt was still Jeremy's best friend. She took this as a good opportunity to bring him up.

"There is something else I have to tell you." She felt her stomach turning and her palms growing sweaty. As he looked at her and waited for her to continue, she didn't know if she'd be able to say it.

"I kissed Matt," she said.

He lifted his eyebrows. "Wow." His tone was flat.

She didn't know what she was expecting. Had she expected him to find the biggest rock at the lake and chuck it into the water like a madman? Did she expect him to start crying? Did she expect him to spit on her? She hadn't really expected him to just sit there, silent. She had no idea what he was thinking.

He finally spoke. "That's kind of a dagger."

"I'm so sorry, Jere. I feel like the worst

person in the world. If you want to hate me, you can. I totally understand."

He tossed another pebble in the water, then looked at her. "Do you like him?"

It took all her courage, but she managed to nod.

"He's a good guy, Nat." Then he squeezed her shoulder. "I won't lie, it hurts. I mean, I don't know . . . he is my best friend."

"I know. I know exactly what you mean."

"I only want the best for you, Nat." He nodded. "And I'd be pissed if you went off and dated some idiot. It's all good."

She smiled. "Thanks."

Jeremy walked her to her car. They gave each other one last hug. He felt warm and familiar, and for a moment she felt a flicker of sadness. It felt similar to the last time she had cleaned out her closet. She'd found her favorite old T-shirt that she'd outgrown five years ago. There were so many good memories, but the truth was she knew she had to let it go. She couldn't hold on to it forever just because there were some great memories. When he pulled away, they looked at each other.

"Still friends?" she asked.

"Always."

Eighteen

It was two days before the dance, and word of the breakup had spread across campus like wildfire. *Natalie had been dumped for Brianna. Brianna had torn their relationship apart.* None of the rumors were true. Strangely, there were bigger headlines in the school tabloids. People were far more interested in Natalie's singing ticket. It was one of those odd little stories that people exchanged while waiting at the bus stop or standing in line at the cafeteria. No one had ever heard of anyone getting a ticket for singing.

In spite of the breakup, everyone wanted to know about her getting pulled over, and specifically what song she'd been singing. She'd since learned that it was called "Big

Girls Don't Cry," which was just completely ironic. Every time she heard Matt's name, she felt like bursting into tears.

Jeremy was still popular and sought after by practically every girl on campus.

Natalie, Jeremy, and Brianna were still friends. The three of them still walked to lunch every day together, and it was actually kind of funny to see the expressions some of their classmates wore when they noticed them laughing and acting as though nothing had ever happened.

Brianna had been worried about going to the dance with Jeremy and had even asked Natalie if it was okay before she accepted his invitation. Natalie had given her full support.

It felt good to be free, but at the same time Natalie felt like things weren't completely resolved. Matt had never replied to her text, and she wasn't even sure if he'd shown up for school again today. He'd been MIA all week. Jo and Vincent had reminded her that he was sick. Rumors were flying that he had mono, which only added to Natalie's stress. What if she had mono?

Today, instead of walking to lunch with Jeremy and Brianna, Natalie took a different route. It was Thursday, which meant that the paper hit stands today. She quickly headed to the nearest stack of newspapers she could find. She gasped with delight when she noticed Matt's ghost story featured on the cover. The newspaper's artist had even sketched a cool, ghostly looking cowboy next to the story.

Mr. Moore must've really liked Matt's story too, because he was the one who decided what made the cover of the newspaper. She read Matt's story for the second time and felt as though it were her own story that had made the cover. She was truly excited for him. She didn't care if all her classmates wondered why she was grinning ear to ear over a ghost story.

After she finished reading the story, she took a moment to look over the paper. She stood next to the newspaper stack while her classmates bustled in next to her, reaching for their copies of the *Coyote Chronicle*.

She became lost inside the pages, oblivious to the world around her as she looked at all the hard work she'd contributed to this particular issue. Seeing her name in a byline felt so rewarding, but in some ways she also felt sad. She'd worked closely with Matt on this issue of the paper, and thinking of their Denny's meetings made her heart ache a little.

Her quiz was featured on the second page of the paper, and the column in its usual place—the last page. She glanced up. Many of her classmates had stopped in their lunch tracks to browse the paper as well. She noticed that a lot of them had already turned to the last page. That silly little column was more popular than anything— even sports. It just went to show how powerful love could be.

Instead of heading to the cafeteria, she headed to the newsroom, holding the paper. She wanted to congratulate Matt on the cover story, and it was about time they resolved a few things—even if it meant the resolution wasn't in her favor. She wasn't looking for a deep conversation or some major breakthrough between them. She just wanted things to be cool. She also had something that she wanted to give him.

She found him sitting in front of the same computer that he always used. He looked up when he noticed her, and she felt her palms turn sweaty. Her copy of the newspaper felt sticky against her hands.

"Hey," she said, "I just wanted to congratulate you. The cover story? That's awesome."

"Thanks," he said. His cheeks turned a little pink as he shrugged. "It's not that big of a deal." His voice wasn't raspy, but he released a little cough.

"Yes, it is!"

"Thanks. I've been meaning to call you."

"Really." She took a step forward. "I hope you're feeling better."

"I am. But it was pretty brutal for a few days there." He cleared his throat. "But listen . . . I just hope . . . everything is cool."

"Of course it is. Um . . ." This was so awkward. "You know I told Jeremy what happened. I hope you're not mad."

"I know. I told him too—that same day, actually. I'm not mad at all . . . I just, I mean, he's my . . ."

"He's your best friend. I know. It's okay." She saved him from telling her what he was really thinking—there was no way he could be with her because his best friend still came first. It was admirable. But it still killed her inside. She sensed sadness in his eyes too. It was so unfair.

There wasn't much more to say, so she

wasted no time and reached into her backpack and pulled out the disk. "Here, it's my latest column. We can use it for November."

He seemed puzzled. "I didn't know that we had decided on—"

"It's from the question you gave me before—the one I didn't answer. I decided to go ahead and write the column anyway. It's my advice."

The corners of his lips turned up, and he seemed a little surprised. He took the disk from her hands. "Thanks, Nat. I look forward to reading it."

"All right, well . . . I'm going to go grab a bite," she said.

"I'll be there in a minute."

She left the newsroom, feeling a combination of relief and sadness. She was relieved their friendship wasn't ruined, but deep in her heart she wanted so much more than his friendship. She sensed he wanted the same.

Nineteen

Dear Stuck Between a Rock and a
Hard Place,
    I bet it really does feel like there is
no way out of your situation. You see, I
know this because I was once in the same
position—stuck between a rock and a
hard place. I can tell you from my own
experience that there is no easy answer
to this question. Keep in mind, the fact
that you are worried about hurting other
people's feelings shows what a good
person you are. You can't help the way
you feel. The only thing you can do in
this particular situation is weigh your
options. Each situation is unique. There
are a thousand maybes. Maybe the people

you think you might be hurting won't be
as hurt as you think they will be. But at
the end of the day, what counts is that you
are honest with yourself. You can't live a
lie. My advice to you is to be honest with
yourself, weigh your options, and at the
end of the day, trust your judgment. You
know what to do.

Wearing her bathrobe, she sat in front of
her computer looking at the column she'd
given to Matt. She knew he'd read it by
now, and she couldn't help but wonder what
he thought. She'd read the column so many
times she practically knew it by heart. She
closed out her screen. She could hear Prints
William going ballistic downstairs, and
knew her friends had probably arrived.

It was time to slip into her costume. As
she pulled the gown over her head, she wondered if Matt was going to the dance. She
hadn't spoken to him since she'd given him
the column. Jo and Vincent hadn't heard
anything.

It wasn't dark yet, and her parents were
helping her brothers get ready. They were
all going trick-or-treating, and Grandma
Jones would pass out candy. Grandma Jones

was watching *Nancy Grace* downstairs. The television was so loud she was afraid that the neighbors would call the police. Grandma Jones would never hear the doorbell ring. Natalie made a mental note to ask for a television for Christmas. Maybe she could have her own small TV in her room, just to escape the freakish shows that Grandma Jones watched.

"Natalie," her mother called. "Jo and Vincent are here."

Natalie found her family and friends downstairs. Brandon had already painted his face white and slicked his hair back. Black circles surrounded his eyes and fake blood dripped down his chin. He was going as a vampire. *Dressed to kill,* Natalie thought. Thomas's astronaut costume didn't require makeup. *Dressed for success.*

Natalie immediately showered her friends with compliments. With his drama background, Vincent had been able to use theater makeup for their dead bride and groom costumes, and they looked awesome. They looked like they were straight off the set of a horror movie. The costumes were by far the best Jo and Vincent had ever worn. There was something else going on with them too. Something in their eyes. Natalie couldn't figure out what it was, but they seemed giddy and confident.

"You look hot too," Vincent said.

"You're the perfect Cleopatra," Jo added.

Natalie had decided to finally go as Cleopatra this year. She could do whatever she wanted now that she was single. Brianna had helped her find the costume. Natalie had to admit, she looked pretty good as Cleopatra. She had her black bob and her waiflike figure with her skinny neck. She wore a full-length Egyptian white-and-gold dress and headpiece. Her eye makeup was dark and sultry. She'd even drawn the signature black Cleopatra eyeliner wings off her eyelids. The funny thing was, she couldn't get over the coincidence—how Cleopatra had come between two friends, Julius Caesar and Mark Antony. The only difference between Natalie's and Cleopatra's love lives was that Natalie's two guys were still friends and Natalie was heading to the dance solo. Natalie doubted that Cleopatra ever attended any dances solo.

Natalie's family had taken the news of the breakup well. She'd imagined they'd throw her out in the streets and ask if they could adopt Jeremy in her place. However, her brothers seemed as though they'd already forgotten him, and both her parents had explained they'd broken up with people at her age also.

The plan for the evening was for the three friends to meet with some of Vincent's drama buddies at Friday's for dinner, and then they were heading to the dance. Vincent drove.

There were a few other groups from school at the restaurant, and it was fun seeing all the costumes. Thankfully, there were a few other singletons in their dinner group. She dined with Danica Patrick and Barack Obama. There were two couples from the fifties and sixties. One couple had even come in the fork and spoon getup. Natalie was just glad that she didn't have to wear it.

Their waitress was dressed as Medusa and had two dozen rubber snakes tied to little braids on her head and blood dripping from a fake cut on her neck. She looked pretty cool.

Natalie was partway through her burger when she glanced across the table and noticed that Vincent's arm was slung over Jo's shoulders as if it belonged there. Jo was snuggled into his chest as if she'd resided in that special place forever. They looked like a couple. Had Jo taken her advice? Was she giving him a chance? They looked great together—even dead.

Natalie was so excited for her friends that she could hardly pay attention to her meal after that. It was en route to the car when Jo squeezed Natalie's arm. Vincent had run back inside to use the bathroom.

"I kissed him," Jo whispered.

Natalie's jaw dropped. "Are you serious?"

Jo nodded. "Shhh."

"Oh my gosh, I'm so excited for you guys. You guys are so cute together."

Jo seemed genuinely happy.

The vibe in the car was different on the way to the dance. Natalie felt like she was riding to the dance with a couple and not just a couple of friends. As she sat in the backseat she felt excited for her friends. But she also felt kind of sad. She thought of Matt and wondered what he was doing. Was he thinking of her, too? Or was he totally over it? It just didn't seem right for them to be apart.

Kevin Rudolf's "Let It Rock" had just started when they entered the gym. The dance floor was packed and the lighting was dim. The Howl at the Moon decor was the best Natalie had ever seen. Jo had won her battle with the decorations and a gigantic yellow moon with a dark blue background hung in the front of the gym. A witch complete with broomstick dangled in front of the moon. Black lights alternated with dim lights, and her classmates' teeth and eyes flashed and glowed. In spite of the party mood, Natalie still felt sad. She couldn't stop thinking about Matt. But what more could she do? She'd given him the column. He had to know how she felt.

Jeremy and Brianna greeted her with hugs. They were dressed as a doctor and a nurse. Jeremy was the nurse. He'd crossed genders and his costume was hilarious. He wore lipstick and a wig, and had stuffed his little nurse dress with fake boobs. Laughing with him felt good.

Jeremy probably knew where Matt was, but she wasn't about to ask him. That would just be too weird.

"You look great, Nat," Jeremy said. "And Jo and Vincent?" He pointed to them. They were holding hands. "What's up with that?" He grinned.

Natalie nodded. "It's about time, right?"

"I'd say so."

She danced a few songs with her friends before deciding she needed some fresh air. She felt disappointed, and her headpiece was starting to give her a headache. Part of her knew Matt wouldn't show up. But she'd been hoping he would. She'd never imagined that his absence would make her so sad. She was heading for the double doors of the gym when a figure appeared in the doorway.

Her heart skipped a beat. She had to move closer just to make sure it was actually him. "Matt?" She hoped she sounded calm and normal. Her heart was pounding so hard she thought it was going to pop right out of her chest.

"Hey, Nat."

Shock rippled through her veins. She gave him a once-over. He had the Caesar hair, but his attire was more Mark Antony. "You're . . . Julius Caeser? Or Mark Antony?"

He shrugged and smiled. "I'm not sure. I just drove around town for three hours looking for one of these, and this was the only one I could find. It wasn't in the package. I just wanted to match you, Nat."

"How did you know?"

"Jo told me."

She laughed and threw her arms around his neck.

"I can't stop thinking about you," he whispered.

"Me too."

They looked at each other beneath the glow of the moon, and in one heartbeat they both leaned in. His kiss felt so warm again, and this time, as she fell into his arms, she knew she didn't have to pull away.

Twenty

Member: Dragon Guy
Advanced Member
RE: A huge dilemma
So, I'm still waiting. Did you stir up enough drama to make those psychos on *The Hills* look normal or what?

Member: Glamour Girl
Advanced Member
RE: A huge dilemma
What's going on, Up All Night? I'm starting to get worried about you. Is everything okay?

Member: Skater Chick
Newbie
RE: A huge dilemma

Hopefully, she's one of the lucky ones. Hopefully, she had a good outcome and is hanging out with her new man.

"Natalie," her mother called. "Vincent and Jo are here!"

"Just a sec!" she yelled back.

She could hear her friends chatting with Grandma Jones about the dance, and what dances were like back in her day. Natalie knew she had a few minutes before Matt arrived.

It had been a week since Howl at the Moon, and a lot had changed. She spent almost every free moment she had with Matt, and had neglected Romeohelpme. Today they were going to the beach for lunch with Jo and Vincent. It was the first time they had doubled, and they were all meeting at Natalie's house. Jo and Vincent were so cute together. Jo had explained that night after the dance that she just felt something inside herself—something that had said, Why not? What was she afraid of? So she'd made the first move with Vincent. They weren't committed for life, but they were trying things out, and so far it seemed to be going very well.

She heard Matt's car in the driveway, and she peeked out her window. He was holding a bouquet of sunflowers. God, he was cute. She spun around and quickly hit her keyboard.

Member: Up All Night
Advanced Member
RE: A huge dilemma
All I want to say for now is this. When things are meant to be they always have a way of working out. Happy endings don't just exist in the movies.

For once, she felt like she knew the answers.

About the Author

Whitney Lyles is the author of *Always the Bridesmaid*, *Here Comes the Bride*, *First Comes Love*, *Roommates*, and the YA romantic comedy *Party Games*. She'll never tell if she had a crush on someone off-limits, but she does admit to some pretty wild Halloween costumes.

Whitney lives with her husband and children in San Diego, California. Visit her on the Web at whitneylyles.com or myspace.com/whitney_lyles.

seat belt
(sēt' belt) *n.* **1.** a trick in which a snowboarder
reaches across the body and grabs the board while
getting air **2.** what Hayden needs to fasten, because
Nick is about to take her for a ride

At the groan of a door opening, I looked
up from my chemistry notebook. I'd been
diagramming molecules so I wouldn't have
any homework to actually take home. But as
I'd stared at the white paper, it had dissolved
into a snowy slalom course. The hydrogen
and oxygen atoms had transformed into gates
for me to snowboard between. My red pen
had traced my path, curving back and forth,
swish, swish, swish, down the page. I could
almost feel the icy wind on my cheeks and
smell the pine trees. I couldn't *wait* to get out
of school and head for the mountain.

Until I saw it was Nick coming out the
door of Ms. Abernathy's room and into the
hall. At six feet tall, he filled the doorway

with his model-perfect looks and cocky attitude. He flicked his dark hair out of his eyes with his pinkie, looked down at me, and grinned brilliantly.

My first thought was, *Oh no: fuel for the fire*. About a month ago, one of my best friends hooked up with one of Nick's best friends. Then, a few weeks ago, my other best friend and Nick's other best friend got together. It was fate. Nick and I were next, right?

Wrong. Everybody in our class remembered that Nick and I had been a couple four years ago, in seventh grade. They gleefully recalled our breakup and the resulting brouhaha. They watched us now for our entertainment value, dying to know whether we'd go out again. Unfortunately for them, they needed to stick to DVDs and Wii to fill up their spare time. Nick and I weren't going to happen.

My second thought was, *Ah, those deep brown eyes*.

Maybe snowboarding could wait a little longer, after all.

"Fancy meeting you here, Hoyden." He closed the door behind him, too hard. He must have gotten in trouble for talking again, and Ms. Abernathy had sent him out in the hall.

Join the club. From my seat against the cement block wall of our high school's science wing, I gazed up at him—way, *way* up, because I was on the floor—and tried my best to glare. The first time he'd called me *Hoyden*, years ago, I'd sneaked a peek in the dictionary to look up what it meant: a noisy girl. Not exactly flattering. Not exactly a lie, either. But I couldn't let him know I felt flattered that he'd taken the time to look up a word in the dictionary to insult me with. Because that would make me insane, desperate, and in unrequited love.

He slapped his forehead. "*Oh*, I'm sorry, I meant *Hayden*. I get confused." He had a way of saying "oh" so innocently, like he had no idea he'd insulted me. Sometimes new girls bought his act, at least for their first few weeks at our school. They were taken by the idea of hooking up with Nick Krieger, who occasionally was featured in teen heartthrob magazines as the heir to the Krieger Meats and Meat Products fortune. And Nick obliged these girls—at least for a few dates, until he dumped them.

I knew his pattern all too well. When I'd first moved to Snowfall, Colorado, I had *been* one of those girls. He'd made me feel like a princess for a whole month. No, better—like a cool, hip teenage girl who dated! The fantasy culminated with one deep kiss shared in the back row of the movie theater with half our English class watching us. It didn't end well, thus the aforementioned brouhaha.

I blinked the stars out of my eyes. "Fancy seeing *you* here, Ex."

He gave me his smile of sexy confidence, dropped his backpack, and sank to the floor beside me. "What do you think of Davis and Liz?"

My heart had absolutely no reason to skip a beat. He was *not* asking me out. He was asking me my opinion of my friend Liz and his friend Davis as a couple. That did not necessarily mean he was heeding public opinion that he and I were next to get together. Liz and Davis were a legitimate topic of gossip.

I managed to say breezily, "Oh, they'll get along great until they discuss where to go on a date. Then he'll insist they go where she wants to go. She'll insist they go where *he* wants to go. They'll end up sitting in her driveway all night, fighting to the death over who can be more thoughtful and polite."

Nick chuckled, a low rumble in his chest. Because he'd sat down so close to me and our arms were touching, sort of, under layers and layers of clothing, I felt the vibration of his voice. But again, my heart had no reason—repeat, *no* reason—to skip two beats, or possibly three, just because I'd made Nick laugh. He made everybody feel this good about their stupid jokes, from the most popular girl in our class down to the chick with straight hair and bottle glasses who wore long denim skirts with her Nikes.

"And what's up with Gavin and Chloe?" he asked next.

"Chloe and Gavin are an accident waiting to happen." I couldn't understand this mismatch between the class president and the class bad boy, and it was a relief finally to voice my concerns, even if it *was* to Nick. "They're both too strong-willed to make it together long. You watch. They're adorable together now, but before long they'll have an argument that makes our tween-love

Armageddon look like a happy childhood memory."

Suddenly it occurred to me that I'd said way too much, and Nick would likely repeat this unflattering characterization to Gavin, who would take it right back to Chloe. I really did hold this opinion of Chloe and Gavin's chances at true love, but I'd never intended to share it! I lost my inhibitions when I looked into Nick's dark eyes, damn him.

I slid my arm around him conspiratorially—not as titillating as it sounds, because his parka was very puffy—and cooed, "But that's just between you and me. I know how good you are at keeping secrets."

He pursed his lips and gazed at me reproachfully for throwing our seventh-grade history in his face, times two. Back then he'd brought our tween-love Armageddon on himself by letting our whole class in on his secret while he kept me in the dark.

Not that I was bitter.

But instead of jabbing back at me, he slipped his arm around me, too. And I was *not* wearing a puffy parka, only a couple of T-shirts, both of which had ridden up a little in the back. I knew this without looking because I felt the heat of his fingers on my bare skin, above the waistband of my jeans. My face probably turned a few shades redder than my hair.

"Now, Hoyden," he reprimanded me. "Valentine's Day is a week from tomorrow. We don't want to ruin that special day for Gavin and Chloe or Davis and Liz. We should put aside our differences for the sake of the kids."

I couldn't help bursting into unladylike laughter.

I expected him to remove his hand from my hip in revulsion at my outburst, but he kept it there. I knew he was only toying with me, I *knew* this, but I sure did enjoy it. If the principal had walked by just then and sensed what I was thinking, I would have gotten detention.

"Four years is a long time for us to be separated," he crooned. "We've both had a chance to think about what we really want from our relationship."

This was true. Over the four years since we'd been together, I'd come to the heartbreaking realization that no boy in my school was as hot as Nick, nobody was as much fun, and nobody was nearly as much of an ass.

For instance, he'd generated fire-crotch comments about me as I passed his table in the lunchroom yesterday.

Remember when another heir called a certain red-haired actress a fire-crotch on camera? No? Well, *I* remember. Redheads across America sucked in a collective gasp, because we *knew*. The jokes boys made to us about Raggedy Ann, the Wendy's girl, and Pippi Longstocking would finally stop, as we'd always hoped, but only to be replaced by something infinitely worse.

So when I heard *fire-crotch* whispered in the lunchroom, I assumed it was meant for me. Nick was the first suspect I glanced at. His mouth was closed as he listened to the conversation at the lunch table. However, when there was commentary around school about me, Nick was always in the vicinity. He might not have made the comment, but I knew in my heart he was responsible.

I chose not to relay my thoughts on our four-year-long trial separation, lest he take his warm hand off my hip. Instead, I played along. "Are you saying you didn't sign the papers, so our divorce was never finalized?"

"I'm saying maybe we should call off the

court proceedings and try a reconciliation."
A strand of his dark hair came untucked from behind his ear, and he jerked his head back to swing the hair out of his eyes. Oooh, I *loved* it when he did that! I had something of a Nick problem.

His hair fell right back into his eyes. Sometimes when this happened, he followed up the head jerk with the pinkie flick, but not this time. He watched me, waiting for me to say something. Oops. I'd forgotten I was staring at him in awe.

A reconciliation? Probably he was just teasing me, as usual. But what if this was his veiled way of asking me on a date? What if he was feeling me out to see whether I wanted to go with him before he asked me directly? This was how Nick worked. He had to win. He never took a bet that wasn't a sure thing.

And if he'd been listening to everyone in class prodding him to ask me out, the timing was perfect, if I did say so myself. He was between girlfriends (not that I kept up with his dating status) and therefore free to get together with me. Everett Walsh, my boyfriend of two months, had broken up with me last week because his mama thought I was brazen (no!). Therefore

I was free to get together with Nick.

Playing it cool, I relaxed against the wall and gave his poofy parka a squeeze, which he probably couldn't feel through the padding. With my other hand, I found his fingers in his lap and touched the engraving on his signet ring, which he'd told me back in seventh grade was the Krieger family crest. It depicted blood-thirsty lions and the antlers of the hapless deer they'd attacked and devoured—which seemed apt for our relationship in seventh grade, but *not* for our relationship now, in eleventh. I was no deer in the headlights. Not anymore. Coyly I said, "I'll mention it to my lawyer." Ha!

He eyed me uneasily, like I was a chemistry lab experiment gone awry and foaming over. But Nick was never truly uneasy. He was just taken aback that I hadn't fallen at his feet. Then he asked, "What are you doing for winter break?"

Winter break was next week. We lived in a ski resort town. It seemed cruel to lock us up in school the *entire* winter. They let us out for a week every February, since the base might or might not start to melt by spring break in April.

Was he just making convo, whiling away our last few minutes of incarceration at school, or did he really want to know what I was doing during our days off? Again I got the distinct and astonishing impression that he wanted to ask me out. Perhaps I should notify Ms. Abernathy of a safety hazard in her chemistry classroom. Obviously I had inhaled hallucinatory gas just before she kicked me out.

"I'm boarding with my brother today," I said, counting on my fingers. "Tomorrow I'm boarding with Liz. Actually, Liz skis rather than boards, but she keeps up with me pretty well. I'm boarding with some friends coming from Aspen on Sunday, the cheerleading squad on Monday—"

Nick laughed. "Basically, anyone who will board with you."

"I guess I get around," I agreed. "I'm on the mountain a lot. Most people get tired of boarding after a while, which I do not understand at *all*. And then on Tuesday, I've entered that big snowboarding competition."

"Really!" He sounded interested and surprised, but his hand underneath my hand let me know he was more interested in throwing me into a hot tizzy than in anything I had to say. He slid his hand, and my hand with it, from his lap and over to my thigh. "You're going off the jump? Did you get over your fear of heights?"

So he'd been listening to me after all.

My friends knew I'd broken my leg rappelling when I was twelve. That actually led, in a roundabout way, to my family's move from Tennessee to Colorado. My dad was a nurse, and he got so interested in my physical rehab that he and my mom decided to open a health club. Only they didn't think they could make it fly in Tennessee. The best place for a privately owned health club specializing in physical rehab was a town with a lot of rich people and broken legs.

Though my own leg had healed by the time we moved, I was still so shell-shocked from my fall that I never would have tried snowboarding if my parents hadn't made me go with my little brother, Josh, to keep him from killing himself on the mountain. Josh was a big part of the reason I'd gotten pretty good. *Any* girl would get pretty good trying to keep up with a boy snowboarder three years younger who was half insane.

And that's how I became the world's only snowboarder with the ability to land a frontside 900 in the half-pipe *and* with a crippling fear of heights. Not a good combination if I wanted to compete nationally.

"This competition's different," I said. Growing warmer, I watched his fingers massaging the soft denim of my jeans. "For once, the only events are the slalom and the half-pipe. No big air or slopestyle or anything that would involve a jump. Chloe and Liz swore they'd never forgive me if I didn't enter this one."

"You've got a chance," Nick assured me. "I've seen you around on the slopes. You're good compared with most of the regulars on the mountain."

I shrugged—a small, dainty shrug, not a big shrug that would dislodge his hand from my hip and his other hand from my thigh. "Thanks, but I expect some random chick from Aspen to sweep in and kick my ass." And when that happened, I sure could use someone to comfort me in the agony of defeat, *hint hint*. But Nick was only toying with me. Nick was only toying with me. I could repeat this mantra a million times in my head, yet no matter how strong my willpower, his fingers rubbing across my jeans threatened to turn me into a nervous gigglefest. Sometimes I wished I were one of those cheerleaders/prom queens/rich socialite snowbunnies who seemed to interest Nick for a day or two at a time. I wondered if any of them had given in to Nick's fingers rubbing across their jeans, and whether I would too, if he asked.

"Anyway, those are all my plans so far," I threw in there despite myself. What I meant was: I am free for the rest of the week, *hint hint*. I wanted to kick myself.

"Are you going to the Poseur concert on Valentine's Day?" He eased his hand out from under mine and put his on top. His fingers massaged my fingers ever so gently.

Nick was only toying with me. Nick was only toying with me. "That's everybody's million-dollar question, isn't it?" I said. "Or rather, their seventy-two-dollar question. I don't want to pass up a once-in-a-lifetime opportunity to see Poseur, but tickets are so expensive." I may have spoken a bit too loudly so he could hear me over my heart, which was no longer skipping beats. It was hammering out a beat faster than Poseur's drummer.

Nick nodded. "Especially if you're buying two because you want to ask someone to go with you."

I gaped at him. I know I did. He watched me with dark, supposedly serious eyes while I gaped at him in shock. Was he laughing at me inside?

We both started as the door burst open. Ms. Abernathy glowered down at us with her fists on her hips. "Miss O'Malley. Mr. Krieger. When I send you into the hall for talking, you do not *talk* in the *hall*!"

"*Oh,*" Nick said in his innocent voice.

I was deathly afraid I would laugh at this if I opened my mouth. I absolutely could not allow myself to fall in love with Nick all over again. But it was downright impossible to avoid. He bent his head until Ms. Abernathy couldn't see his face, and he winked at me.

Saved by the bell! We all three jumped as the signal rang close above our heads. On a normal day the class would have flowed politely around Ms. Abernathy standing in the doorway. They might even have waited until she moved. But this bell let us out of school for winter break. Ms. Abernathy got caught in the current of students pouring out of her classroom and down the hall. If she floated as far as the next wing, maybe a history teacher would throw her a rope and tow her to safety.

Chloe and Liz shoved their way out of the room and glanced around the crowded hall until they saw me against the wall on the floor. Clearly they were dying to know whether I'd survived being sent out in the hall with my ex. Both of them focused on the space between me and Nick. I looked down in confusion, wondering what they were staring at.

Nick was still holding my hand.

I tried to pull my hand away. He squeezed even tighter. I turned to him with my eyes wide. What in the world was he thinking? After the insults Nick and I had thrown at each other in public over the years, we would have been the laughingstock of the school if we *really* fell for each other.

And now he was holding my hand in public!

He wouldn't look at me, though I pulled hard to free myself from his grasp. He just squeezed my hand and grinned up at the gathering crowd like he didn't care who saw us.

Which was *everyone*. Davis sauntered out of the classroom and slid his arm around Liz. Unlike the train wreck that was Chloe and Gavin as a couple, Liz and Davis were the two kindest people I knew. They deserved each other, in a good way. But even Davis had a comment as he casually glanced down at Nick and me and did a double take at our hands. "That's something you don't see every day," he understated to Liz. "Usually at about this time, Nick is going around the lab, collecting whatever particulate has dropped out of the solution so he can throw it at Hayden."

"We didn't do an experiment today, just diagrammed molecules. Nothing to throw," Nick said in a reasonable tone, as if he and I were not sitting on the floor, surrounded by a two-deep crowd of our classmates. They had all filed out of chemistry class and joined the circle, peeking over one another's shoulders to see what Nick and I were up to this time.

Then Gavin exploded out of the classroom, and I knew Nick and I were in trouble. He whacked into Chloe so hard, he would have knocked her off her feet if he hadn't grabbed her at the same time. Over her squeals, he yelled at Nick, "I knew it!" while pointing at our hands.

"Oooooh," said the crowd, shifting closer around us, totally forgetting they were supposed to be *going home* for *winter break*. If Davis, Liz, Gavin, and Chloe hadn't made up the front row, the rest of the class would have overrun us like zombies.

"I was just shaking Hayden's hand, wishing her luck in the snowboarding competition Tuesday." Nick stood, still gripping my hand, pulling me up with him.

"See you tonight," Davis mouthed in Liz's ear. Then he turned to Nick and said, "Come on. I'll fill you in on what Ms. Abernathy said after you got ejected from the game." Of course Nick didn't give a damn what Ms. Abernathy said in the last ten minutes of class before winter break. But that was Davis, always smoothing things over.

Nick *finally* let go of my hand. "See you around, Hoyden." He pinned me with one last dark look and a curious smile. Then he and Davis made their way through the crowd, shoving some of the more obnoxious gawking boys, who elbowed them back.

But a few folks still stared at me: Liz,

Chloe, and worst of all, Gavin. One corner of his mouth turned up in a mischievous grin. Gavin was tall, muscular, and Japanese, with even longer hair than Nick. I would have thought he was adorable if I didn't want to kill him most of the time for constantly goading Nick and me about each other. I certainly understood what Chloe saw in him, even though he drove her crazy too.

Gavin turned to her. "Give me some gum."

"No."

Liz and I dodged out of the way as Gavin backed Chloe against the lockers and shoved both his hands into the front pockets of her jeans. You might think the class president would find a way to stop this sort of man-handling, but actually she didn't seem to mind too much.

By now the crowd had dispersed. Nick and Davis were walking down the hall together, getting smaller and smaller until I couldn't see them anymore past a knot of freshman girls squealing about the Poseur concert and how they were working extra shifts at the souvenir shop to pay for the expensive tickets. Go home, people. I resisted the urge to stand on my tiptoes for one more peek at Nick. If I didn't run into him on the slopes, this might be the last I saw of him for ten whole days.

"I don't have any gum!" Chloe squealed through fits of giggling, trying to push Gavin off. "Gavin!" She finally shoved him away.

He jogged down the hall to catch up with Nick and Davis, holding the paper-wrapped strip of gum aloft triumphantly.

"That was my last piece!" Chloe called.

I never would have admitted that Gavin's gum theft made me jealous. Nick was bad for me, I knew. He was the last person on earth I wanted to steal my gum. Still, I stepped to one side so I could see him behind the Poseur fangirls. I watched him turn with Gavin and Davis and disappear down the stairs, and I couldn't help but feel like a little kid on Halloween night, standing in the doorway in my witch costume with my plastic cauldron for trick-or-treat candy, watching the rain come down. Such sweet promise, and now I was out of luck. Damn.

Chloe stared after the boys too. I assumed she really wanted that gum. Then she looked at me. "Oh my God, did Nick ask you out?

It sounded like he was asking you out, but we couldn't quite tell. Ms. Abernathy finally came to check on you because the whole first row got up from their desks and pressed their ears to the door."

I answered honestly. "For a second there, I thought he was going to ask me out."

"But he didn't?" Liz wailed.

To hide my disappointment, I bent down to stuff my chemistry notebook into my backpack as I shook my head.

"At least you got a *see you around*," Chloe pointed out. "Normally if he bothered to say good-bye to you at all, he would do it by popping your bra."

"True," I acknowledged. And then I realized what was going on here. Chloe and Liz had been hinting that I should go out with Nick now that they were dating Nick's friends, but at the moment they seemed even more eager and giddy about it than usual. I straightened, folded my arms across my chest, and glared at Chloe and then Liz. "Please do not tell me you put Nick up to asking me to the Poseur concert."

Chloe stared right back at me. But Liz, the weakest link, glanced nervously at Chloe like they were busted.

"Come on now." I stamped one foot. "Even y'all aren't going to the Poseur concert with Gavin and Davis. It's too expensive."

"Nick has more money than God," Chloe pointed out.

I turned on Liz. "You really want me to go out with him after I told you he made that fire-crotch comment about me?" Liz was all about people being respectful of one another. We were in school with teenage boys and this was asking a lot, I know.

"That *did* sound disrespectful," she admitted. "Are you sure he didn't mean it in a friendly way?"

Incredible. Even Liz's sense of chivalry and honor was crushed under the juggernaut called Wouldn't It Be Cute/Ironic If Nick and Hayden Dated Again.

"What if he *did* ask you out?" Liz bounced excitedly, and her dark curls bounced with her. "Oh my God, what if you saw him on the slopes over the break and he asked you to the Poseur concert? What would you say?"

I considered this. Part of me wanted to think Nick had changed in the past four years. I would jump at the chance to go out with the boy I'd made up in my head. In real life Nick was adorable, funny, and smart, but in my fantasies he had the additional fictional component of honestly wanting to go out with me.

Another part of me remembered his dis four years ago as freshly as if it were yesterday. When I recalled that awful night, the image of Honest Nick dissolved, even from my imagination. That Nick was too good to be true. I couldn't say yes to Nick, because I was scared to death he would hurt me again.

"It doesn't matter," I declared, "because he's not going to ask me out. If he really liked me, he wouldn't have treated me the way he did back in the day. So stop trying to throw us together."

"Okay," Liz and Chloe said in unison. Again, too eager, too giddy. The three of us turned and made our own way down the hall. We discussed how low Poseur tickets would have to go before we sprung for them, but the subject had changed too easily. I was left with the nagging feeling that, despite their promise, they were not through playing Cupid with me and Nick.

Want to hear what the Romantic Comedies authors are doing when they are not writing books?

Check out PulseRoCom.com to see the authors blogging together, plus get sneak peeks of upcoming titles!

Nothing can stand in their way . . . except their own dark secrets.

Need a distraction?

Julie Linker

Amy Belasen & Jacob Osborn

Anita Liberty

Charity Tahmaseb & Darcy Vance

Eileen Cook

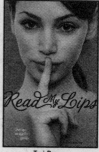

Teri Brown

From Simon Pulse
Published by Simon & Schuster

Check Your Pulse

Simon & Schuster's **Check Your Pulse** e-newsletter offers current updates on the hottest titles, exciting sweepstakes, and exclusive content from your favorite authors.

Visit **SimonSaysTEEN.com** to sign up, post your thoughts, and find out what every avid reader is talking about!

Margaret K. McElderry Books

Simon & Schuster
Books for Young Readers

SIMON PULSE